Crashing on Ballyhoo

It was a long, long fall for the little Space Angel. She fell for miles ████ ʼck of space, past the little, silvery moon and into the atmosphere of the rʼ ████ ʼver to land on. Ballyhoo.

The protective bubble around Juliet began to glow red hɔ ████ ʌe air, while inside it she began to sweat as she fumbled with an open box attacɩ ████ ʌside the box was a large, glowing crystal connected to a tangle of light circuits.

"Oh, come on, please," she was muttering to herself, very scaɪ ʌ now, as she prodded and poked at the insides of the box. "Just a little more time now, that's all I need."

But she knew that time was what she didn't have. Below her the ground was rushing up closer at a frightening rate and Juliet knew that even the bubble wouldn't save her if she hit the ground at such a speed.

"Yes!" she cried out triumphantly, closing the repaired box and sealing it by running her finger along the edge. She twisted, rolled over and thought hard.

BOOM!

There was a huge crash and roar as Juliet's enormous wings of golden light appeared. But it was too late, she was too close and too fast; the wings slowed her down but couldn't stop her.

The Space Angel hit the tree tops at a slight angle, went through them like a missile and roared straight into the slimy mud at the bottom of a shallow lake. The water boiled and a plume of steam whistled up into the air like a giant kettle that was bubbling over.

As Juliet fainted, from the heat, the fear and the terrible forces that slammed into her body when she hit the ground. the golden bubble disappeared. Water rushed over her and she sank with a plop! face first into the mud.

Stolen Fanglefitch

"Ooohh, it hurts!" Juliet groaned as she began to wake up.

"Tell me where it hurts," a voice said gently.

Instantly the angel was wide awake and terrified. She opened her eyes and nearly screamed but managed to stop herself. She was looking into the face of a little boy who seemed no older than herself and not very much different. He certainly didn't seem like he was about to eat her for breakfast.

"Where does it hurt?" he asked again, his dark brown eyes worriedly searching her sparkling blue ones. "Can you move?"

Juliet sat up carefully. She ached everywhere and her head was pounding but nothing seemed to be broken.

"I'm okay," she told the boy. "Where am I?"

"By the shore of Big Puddle Lake," he answered. She looked confused and he smiled, "I pulled you out."

The Space Angel looked down at herself and wrinkled her nose in dismay. She was soaking wet, covered in sticky, smelly mud and her beautiful, blue starshine dress was ruined.

"It may only be a big puddle," she said solemnly, "but that's enough to drown in. Thank you for saving my life." She looked at the boy and smiled and tried to touch him with her mind.

Nothing happened.

She tried again.

Nothing happened. Again.

"My fanglefitch has gone," she cried in horror, looking down to where the box should have been.

"What," the boy grinned as if waiting for the punch line to a joke, "is a fanglefitch?"

"It's ... that is ... I mean ... " Juliet stopped, remembering that she wasn't at home.

"It's a box," she said at last, "about this big," she showed him with her hands, "and it clips onto my belt. It's very important."

"Perhaps it fell off in the water," he suggested.

"No!" Juliet said sharply and shook her head. The she wished that she hadn't as it only made the headache worse.

"No, it can't fall off, it must have been taken off." She looked at the boy suspiciously, "did you ... ?"

"How dare you?" he answered with quiet anger. "I didn't take anything from you. I pull you out of the water, save your life and now you accuse me of stealing!" He stood up and began to walk away.

"Wait!" Juliet called after him. He stopped but did not turn around. She struggled to her feet, became dizzy and nearly fell over but caught her balance and stood up straight.

"I'm sorry," she told him, "I didn't mean it, I'm just scared. Without the fanglefitch I can't get home and I can't call anyone for help. Can we start again?"

Reluctantly the boy turned around, trying to keep a sullen look on his face but a cheeky smile kept on breaking through.

"My name is Juliet. Thank you for saving my life."

"My name is Mega Trix," the boy replied, letting the smile stay, "and saving you was my pleasure."

Juliet smiled back and the two of them didn't say anything for a while. Then another wave of dizziness hit Juliet and she began to fall over. Mega Trix jumped forward and caught her.

"Are you all right?" he asked and felt stupid because he could see that she wasn't.

"I feel giddy and sick, and my head is throbbing," she told him, "apart from that I feel fine."

"Come on," he put an arm around her waist and she put an arm around his shoulders, "we'll go to my house and get you fixed up." Juliet kindly allowed him to help her.

Mega Trix Faircon O'Neill

It didn't take the two of them very long to reach the village of Fair Trade Inc., despite the fact that Juliet was leaning very heavily on Mega Trix.

It was a pretty little village of about a hundred stone cottages with thatched roofs. The community hall or village hall at the centre was a much larger, round building with several large satellite dishes on top. The streets of the village radiated out from this building like the spokes of a wheel and were filled with horse-drawn carts, children and adults walking or cycling, laughing, smiling people. A picture of a happy community.

So why was Mega Trix sneaking Juliet down little alleyways, trying to keep her out of sight?

"In here, quickly," Mega ushered Juliet though a door and into one of the cottages. "Mum!" he called out, "Dad! Where are you?"

"Mega Trix, what is all this fuss and noise about?" a woman's voice replied, sounding annoyed and resigned at the same time. "Your father is at the meeting ..." she fell silent as she stepped out into the hall and saw Juliet.

Mega Trix's mother was a tall woman, with dark and large brown eyes. She had the look of kindliness and over-stretched patience that mothers of young boys everywhere seem to have, with the usual worries about what trouble her son has been causing.

"What happened?" she demanded, sweeping Juliet into her arms and marching off to the bathroom. "What have you done?"

"Aww, mum," Mega's voice whined, "it wasn't me, I didn't do anything wrong. I rescued her."

"Well, all right then," his mother obviously didn't believe him but was too busy to say so. "You go and wait in the front room while I clean her up and see what damage there is. Go on, shoo!"

Miserably, Mega did as he was told, kicking doors, various pieces of furniture and the cat along the way. He knew that somehow, some way, he was going to get blamed for something.

"It's not fair," he mumbled.

"What's not fair?"

Mega jumped at the sound of his father's deep voice and looked up guiltily.

"Well, what is so unfair?" his father asked again, "and why do I have this feeling that it's probably your fault?"

"It's not my fault!" Mega started loudly, "I saved her, I didn't hurt her. Then she was dizzy and ..." he stopped the confused explanation as his mother came into the room.

"You're very lucky my boy," she said to Mega and kissed his father on the cheek, "she isn't hurt, just lots of mud and a few bruises. She's having a shower now."

"Who is not hurt?" Mega's father was beginning to sound annoyed, "and just who is in our shower?"

"Yes, go on Mega," his mother added, "I'd like to know as well."

So Mega Trix Faircon O'Neill had to explain, while being sure that he would get into trouble for something. He just didn't know what yet.

So he told his parents about how he had been wandering through the forest (not saying anything about having been to Forbidden Grotto), when something had rocketed through the trees and crashed with a loud BOOM! into Big Puddle Lake. But by the time he got to the scene all he found was a little girl floating, face down in the water.

" ... and that's all dad, really."

Mega's father looked hard at his son, as if searching for evidence of the lies he knew his son must be telling. The thunder clouds in his face grew darker and more ominous and Mega knew that there was real trouble brewing but still his father hadn't said anything. Then Juliet walked into the room.

"I hope you don't mind me borrowing this robe," she said quietly, "but my dress is filthy."

The three O'Neil's turned to look at Juliet.

"Well, I never ... " said Mega's mother.

"Oh, no!" said Mega's father.

"Wow!" said Mega.

Juliet's long hair was so blond that it was nearly white, her deep, blue eyes were set in a pale, fragile face and her smile glowed like sunshine.

"I'm sorry about all the mud," she apologised, "but it was a lovely shower. Has Mega been telling you about how he saved my life? I really am very grateful you know."

At this point Mega's father stood up, jammed his hands deep into his pockets and paced back and forth, muttering;

"Oh no. Oh no no no. No! Why does it always have to be my son that gets involved. Again and again, if there's trouble around, Mega Trix Faircon O'Neil is at the dead centre of it. Even when he tries to do a good deed he manages to cause never ending trouble for everyone and I ... " he paused to glare at his son, " ... I have to sort it out."

He paced up and down a few more times and then stopped, staring at Juliet.

"You are an angel?" he said, not really asking, "a real, live, honest to goodness Space Angel."

Juliet simply nodded, seeing that he was very upset but not understanding why. Mega was staring at his father with eyes so wide that they nearly popped out of his head.

"Space Angel?" he sputtered, "Space Angel? But they don't exist, they're just stories for children."

"I know son," Mega's father nodded, "I know. They do not exist. Yet here we have one in our house." He turned his attention back to Juliet. "Suppose we start with how you came to be here."

"I crashed," Juliet shrugged her shoulders, "I didn't mean to land here but I couldn't help it. And now someone's taken my fanglefitch and I can't get home." Tears welled up in the little angel's eyes, overflowed and started to trickle down her cheeks. "I didn't want to cause any trouble," she sobbed gently, "it was an accident and now I want my mum and dad but I can't even call them."

"Don't start blubbering ... " Mega's father began but he was too late.

"Shush now, Swindlefair O'Neil," Mega's mother shoved his father aside, "can't you see that the poor child's frightened?" She sat down beside Juliet, comforting her with hugs and soft words.

"She isn't the only one who's frightened!" Lord O'Neill snapped back angrily. "Do you know how much trouble we'll be in if the Wizard Lord finds out that we have a Space Angel in our home? After he personally declared them non-existent? We'll be lucky if he doesn't destroy the entire village. Would you like the Dogs of War to visit us?"

"Well, you are the great Lord Maximus Swindlefair O'Neil," his wife replied, frightened by mention of the Dogs of War but also angry, "manager of Fair Trade Inc., leader of the Multi-Village Corporation. Think of something!"

Lord O'Neill looked at his wife with fear, sadness and anger in his eyes.

"You're right," he agreed heavily, "it's my responsibility to sort it out. And I have to think of the welfare of the whole village. I'll call an emergency meeting of the board and recommend that she be handed over to Vizrah Khan."

Lord Swindlefair O'Neil looked into his wife's eyes with great intensity, trying to say something that he couldn't say in words.

"She had better be here when I get back," he said aloud, "no matter how long I take."

"I understand," Lady O'Neil replied, looking to her husband with equal intensity, "she will be here."

Mega's father turned to leave, pausing only to smile sadly at Juliet.

"But you can't!" Mega Trix protested loudly but his father carried on out and closed the door. "You can't let Khan have her. And she can't be a Space Angel anyway!"

"I am."

"What?" Mega whirled around to Juliet.

"I am," she said again, "a Space Angel. Who is this Khan?"

"Vizrah Khan," Mega growled, "is the Wizard Lord, the Emperor of Ballyhoo. He rules with the help of evil magic and the Dogs of War. He'd probably throw you into the Maze of Fear or the Darkling Pit. Or worse!"

"But why?"

"He doesn't need a reason," Lady O'Neil spoke up, "Mega Trix is right, Khan is evil. You must get away from here right now. Come I'll find you some clothes to wear and then 'Trix will take you into the forest." She smiled at her son, "he knows all the best places to hide. I can never find him when there's work to be done."

Wearing a T-shirt that came down to her knees and a pair of shorts that almost reached her ankles (held up by a piece of string), Juliet followed Mega into the forest. They had left a narrow path and were fighting their way through the trees, which were more like giant bushes with branches starting nearly at ground level, growing out sideways to entangle themselves with the next tree along.

"Come on!" Mega Trix told Juliet impatiently, "we have to get to headquarters before the grown ups start looking for you."

"Headquarters of what?" she asked, lip trembling as yet another twig scratched her arm.

"You'll see," he answered mysteriously, "just hurry up."

So they battled on in silence through the gloomy darkness, the twigs and branches of every tree seeming to deliberately grasp at their clothes, slowing them down, holding them back.

Until, suddenly, Juliet pushed and there was nothing to push against.

"What?" she cried out as she fell flat on the ground. Luckily the floor was covered in soft leaves and moss so all that got bruised this time was her pride as she heard several voices laughing.

"Yes, very funny," she said huffily.

Juliet sat up and folded her arms, trembled her bottom lip and sent a black look at those who had been laughing.

The Space Angel found herself sitting at the edge of a clearing, about ten feet across and maybe five feet high, like a bubble in the dark froth of the forest. In the middle of the clearing, trying hard not to grin, sat Mega Trix and three identical young girls.

"Juliet, meet the Leaping Lonigans," said Mega, "Flip, Slip and Slider meet the Space Angel."

The three girls gasped and looked at her with big, serious eyes.

"How do you do?" said Juliet.

"Fine," the triplets cooed in unison, "are you a real Space Angel?"

Juliet nodded, then added;

"I'm also lonely, scared and a long way from home."

The Lonigans reacted immediately:

"Ah, poor baby," they said and all three went to Juliet and gave her a cuddle.

"Never you mind," said Flip, "we'll help you."

"Of course we will," Slip agreed.

"Were you born in space?" asked Slider.

"No, silly," Juliet was already smiling, "I was born on Dawnlight. It's a planet like this, only a few million miles from here."

"A few million miles?" the triplets had gone back to speaking in unison in their disbelief. Juliet shrugged her shoulders.

"Yeah," she said, "I was just playing around your moon with some friends when I simply lost concentration for a moment and crash landed here."

Juliet noticed the Lonigans were staring at her with wide eyes and gaping mouths.

"It's fantastic," Mega Trix spoke wistfully, "we've only read about space and you're talking about flitting between planets for fun." He shrugged his shoulders as if to apologise for sounding foolish.

"There's nothing very special about going into space," Juliet told them, "if I could get my fanglefitch back I'd take you up and show you."

There was an even more stunned silence.

"You mean that?" Mega asked in a breathless whisper.

"Honestly?" chimed the triplets together.

"Of course," Juliet nodded, "no problem." Her lip started trembling again, "if I can get my fanglefitch back."

"In that case," Mega Trix jumped up and saluted, "you have come to the right place Ma'm. Welcome to the headquarters of Adventures Unlimited."

Juliet looked around the clearing, trying to see something special about it.

"This is headquarters?" she asked doubtfully.

"Naturally," Slider answered, as if it should be obvious to anyone.

"If you don't mind," Mega pushed Slider to one side, "I'll explain. There are hidden clearings like this all over the forest and our gang uses them all. We call them offices and we call ourselves Adventures Unlimited, although we haven't actually had many real adventures so far ..."

"... none at all ..." put in Slider but Mega ignored her and carried on;

"... and this is the biggest clearing so we named it headquarters."

Juliet looked around again but it still looked like a dark and dingy clearing to her, not at all like the head office of an organization or even a gang.

"You really think you can help me?" she asked.

"Of course we can!" shouted Mega and then, more quietly and with a sly smile, "besides, how many adventurers do you know on this planet?"

Juliet grinned sheepishly in reply and Mega Trix bowed low with a flourish, winked at her;

"Shall we get started?" he asked and Juliet nodded.

"Slider, you go round up the rest of the gang and bring 'em here. Flip, we'll need some food and drink, enough to last all of us a few days at least. Slip, you'd better get the survival equipment." When she looked blank Mega explained in a loud whisper, "your Dad's camping gear."

The three girls stood up together, saluted (sort of) and shot off in three different directions, disappearing into the forest like squizzels into a nurgly bush.

Blue Striped Fizzpop

It was nearly an hour before the first of the Leaping Lonigans returned. Juliet had spent most of the time telling Mega Trix about her planet, called Dawnlight, and how all the children there learned to fly through space. Mega was desperate to hear anything she could tell him about space and her voice was beginning to get a little hoarse when Flip Lonigan dropped into the middle of "Headquarters" from the tangled branches above.

"Ignore her," said Mega, "she's just showing off."

With her Flip had two huge rucksacks which she threw triumphantly to the ground.

"Sarnies, cakes, biscuits and fizzpop," she announced.

Almost instantly Mega and Juliet jumped onto the bags and started stuffing their faces with food.

"Hey!" Flip complained, "that was supposed to be for all of us."

Juliet looked up guiltily and stopped but Mega waved at her to carry on.

"Neither of us have had anything for ages," he managed to tell Flip around a mouthful of noodle burger sarnie and blue striped fizzpop. "We can get some more supplies later."

Flip plonked herself down with a "same as usual" look just as Slip returned, dragging a bag as big as herself and apparently just as heavy.

"Give me a hand then," she growled and Flip rushed over to help. "Why do I get all the lousy jobs?" Slip complained and sat down puffing and panting.

"Just lucky, I guess," giggled Mega and Juliet nearly choked when she started laughing as well. Slip glared at the both of them but before she could say anything Slider came back into headquarters.

"Hi everyone," she called out cheerily, "the gang's all here."

Juliet, just finishing the last mouthful of odd job sarnie and gulp of yellow spotted fizzpop, nearly choked again when she saw who, or what, was following Slider.

He was huge. He had to duck his head to stand up in the clearing and his legs seemed as thick as tree trunks. Muscles bulged out all over his arms and even his face seemed to be rippling with muscle.

"Hello," he grinned at her and spoke in a soft, gentle voice, "I'm Slam Dunk."

Juliet nodded silently in return. She had almost regained her composure when the next gang member came through and her mouth dropped open so far her chin nearly hit the floor.

Nearly as tall as Slam Dunk but ultra thin, he moved silently, gliding over the twigs and leaves as if he was hardly touching them. He had two arms and two legs but his face and skin was that of a snake, and every now and again a forked tongue would flick out and quickly back in again. He wore a beautiful suit of dreamsilk that kept changing colour as he moved.

"Hi," he hissed softly at her, "I'm known as The Groover."

The last gang member to come into the clearing was almost disappointingly normal. At least he looked it.

"Good afternoon young lady," he came straight over to Juliet, took hold of her hand and kissed the back of it. "Your troubles are over for I, Anyway, am here. The smartest, strongest, tallest, bravest, and all around most wonderful person on this planet."

Juliet looked more than slightly confused.

"Tallest?" she queried. Unless her eyes were playing tricks on her, Anyway didn't appear to be any taller than herself and certainly nowhere near as tall as Slam Dunk or the Groover.

"Ahem, I, er ..." Mega Trix sounded embarrassed. "He, er ... tells lies."

"But of course," Anyway agreed proudly, "I am the world's greatest liar."

"Is he?" Juliet asked quietly.

"How do we know?" Mega shrugged his shoulders, "he keeps lying."

Deciding to forget about Anyway's lies for the moment, the gang sat themselves down in a semi-circle, loosely focussed on Juliet.

"All right!" Mega Trix called out and clapped his hands three times fast, three times slow and then three times fast again. "We now have the full membership of Adventures Unlimited and we have some important business to discuss ... "

"Perhaps," the Groover interrupted, "more important than you know."

"What do you mean by that?" Mega asked him.

"You have been here all afternoon," the Groover hissed, "so you haven't seen the gogglebox. I was watching it just before Slider arrived to get me and the Wizard Lord himself was on." He paused and everyone leaned forward, a little excited, a little scared. The Groover went on;

"He wanted everyone to look out for a little girl, whose description matches Juliet amazingly well. Anyone who helps her is banished to the Maze of Fear forever and the Dogs of War are combing the countryside for her. Apparently she stole something from him."

The members of Adventures Unlimited looked at each other, their eyes widening slowly as they realized that this, their first adventure, wasn't a game at all. It was totally, seriously serious. Their eyes turned from searching each other's faces and all stared at Juliet.

"Shineola!" Flip Lonigan swore with a great deal of feeling. "This is getting dangerous already. What did you take from him?"

"Nothing," Juliet whispered and shrugged her shoulders. After a few second's thought she allowed her bottom lip to tremble a bit.

"Hey, come on!" Mega Trix put an arm around her shoulders and shot an angry look at the rest of the gang. "It's obviously a lie he's made up just because he wants to get hold of her." He turned to Juliet and squeezed her shoulders. "We won't turn you in or let you down," he assured her, "we're going to help you find that fanglefitch and bat's bums to old Khan."

The rest of the gang gasped in shock and looked around quickly to see if anyone could be listening.

Anyway stood up.

"Anyway," he said, "I'm not afraid of Vizrah Khan. I was telling him just last week that he'd better be careful ... "

"ANYWAY!" shouted the rest of the gang and he looked around, as if surprised that anyone should want to interrupt him.

"Well, that's not really important," he continued, "but what is important is the Searching Stone."

"Anyway," Slam Dunk warned him, "if this is another one of your stories ... "

"Anyway," said Anyway loudly, ignoring Slam, "when slider came to get me I immediately grabbed the Searching Stone. It was given to me by a passing wise man in exchange for me telling him the route to inner peace and tranquillity." He pulled a cheap, tacky looking bracelet out of his pocket, just a tatty, leather strap with what looked like a piece of bluish quartz attached to it.

"That's enough, Anyway," growled Slam Dunk. Anyway began looking around for a quick way out but they were both stopped by Juliet's excited shout;

"A Dream Gem!" she squealed. This wasn't particularly helpful to anyone and only brought about a confused silence. Of course, Anyway was the first to recover.

"Anyway," he began, "as I was saying. This Searching Stone is actually a Dream Gem and naturally I recognised it's usefulness straight away. Juliet," he threw the bracelet to her, "why don't you show them how it works?"

"I don't know," she replied. Her initial happiness had quickly died away and now she sounded uncertain. "This is a very small Gem and I've never used a raw one, without a fanglefitch." Still, she stood up and pressed the blue stone to her forehead.

Juliet squeezed her eyes tight shut and held herself very quiet and still. Everyone waited in an expectant hush. A few moments later, nothing happened. A few more moments after that and nothing happened again. The gang were just about to give up when a glow appeared behind Juliet.

The glow spread out, thinned out, became a sparkling, gossamer light that shaped itself into beautiful, golden wings almost too faint to see. For a second the wings brightened and then, with a sudden whoosh! like a deflating balloon, all the light sucked itself back into a small, golden ball that floated behind Juliet's shoulders.

"It's no good," she was miserable, "I need the fanglefitch. I can't even call for help or hear if anyone's calling me." Still holding the Dream Gem to her head with one hand, Juliet began reaching in front of her, as if searching for something that no one else could see.

"I can hear something though," she told them, "I think it's my fanglefitch, a long way away. There's something else, a noise, like something howling or wailing and moving very fast."

Juliet let both hands fall to her sides then flopped down onto the ground, obviously worn out.

"I can't make head or tail of any of that," she said glumly, "do any of you know what it means?"

She waited for an answer but there wasn't one. Even Anyway stayed silent. After a little while she sat up and looked around at Adventures Unlimited, who were all staring fixedly at the ground.

"What's wrong?" she asked but they all continued staring at the ground. "Mega Trix? Slam

SPACE ANGEL

Dunk? Anyway? Someone tell me what's up."

All the gang looked to Mega Trix as the leader and eventually he looked up, sighed and faced Juliet.

"The fast moving thing making the noise," he explained, "sounds very much like a Banshee Wailer. If a Banshee took your fanglefitch then Khan will have it by now, which means you'll never get it back. I'm sorry Juliet."

She looked at each face in turn and each one turned away from her, feeling a little ashamed but mostly feeling that their first real adventure was slipping away from them before it had even had a chance to begin. The gang started to shuffle back into the forest, out of headquarters, shoulders slumped, feet dragging through the leaves.

"WAIT!" Mega's sudden shout stopped everyone and frightened the life out of Juliet.

"What are we doing?" he asked of no one in particular. "We're leaving this little girl, this Space Angel, alone and lost and frightened. Without our help the Dogs of War will find her and capture her in no time. Then Vizrah Khan will have her and he'll ... that is he ... " Mega's imagination failed him and he finished lamely, " ... do nasty things."

During his little speech Adventures Unlimited had drifted back into headquarters and formed a circle around him.

"But this is real," said Flip.

"This is dangerous," said Slip.

"This is gonna be fun," said Slider, grinning.

"That's right," Mega Trix agreed with all the Triplets, "it's going to be real and dangerous and fun. And I'm going to help Juliet to get her fanglefitch back, even if I have to spit in the Wizard Lord's face." He folded his arms, set his chin and silently challenged the rest of them.

The silence that followed was so deep that you could almost hear everyone thinking. They couldn't let Juliet down and besides, none of them could resist such a challenge.

"All right O'Neil," Slam Dunk was the first to speak up, "I'm not going to let you have all the fun."

"And we'd better come along," said Flip and Slip together, "to look after Slider."

"None of you is going anywhere without me," hissed the Groover.

Again there was a pause as they all turned to look at Anyway, who met their questioning stares with complete calm.

"Anyway," he said, "I was going to help Juliet all along. I was just waiting to see what the rest of you would do."

13

The Road to Nowhere

Daylight was fading and the shadows growing long by the time the adventurers had circled the village and reached the main road north. They peered out uncertainly from behind some trees.

"Here it is," whispered Mega.

"Here's what?" the Space Angel whispered back.

"The road to Nowhere," Groover hissed at her.

"The road to Nowhere?" Juliet repeated the name, puzzled. "Why would anyone build a road to Nowhere?"

All of the gang turned to look at her as if she was very stupid.

"How else would anyone get there?" Slam Dunk asked. Before Juliet could think of a reply, Mega held a finger to his lips and motioned for them all to lay down. They did so and followed his intense stare along the road.

After a few moments they heard a heavy rumbling sound, as if the God of Thunder himself were coming along. Around a bend in the road came a band of huge, scaly creatures trotting along, taking up all the road, knowing that everyone would get out of their way.

Each creature had thick, muscular legs, a long, heavy tail with vicious spikes at the end and a long, narrow head full of sharp teeth. But the creatures weren't the most frightening, it was their riders that made the pit of your stomach twist and turn with fear, that made your skin go cold and clammy and made the hairs stand up on the back of your neck.

Juliet tried to study the riders but her mind wouldn't accept what she was seeing, they were so twisted and warped. When they had passed by all she could remember was lots of fangs, horns, claws and hideously ugly faces. She was shaking with fear just at having seen them.

When they had finally passed out of sight no one said anything for a long time, no one moved, it seemed like no one even breathed.

"The Dogs of War," Mega said eventually. He stood up and breathed deeply. "Come on, we'd better get moving." He set off in the opposite direction to the soldiers and the rest quickly followed.

Before very long daylight had gone completely and they were walking along in total darkness. Or almost total. Juliet noticed that the road itself seemed to be glowing very faintly, just enough so that they could see it.

"Do you know that the road is glowing?" she asked Mega.

"Of course," he replied, "you can always see the road to Nowhere."

They trudged on quietly and miserably for what seemed like days but Juliet knew that it could not have been more than an hour. The small, bright moon was still low in the sky. Apart from the occasional, mournful cry in the forest the only noise was their own footsteps.

"It's here, Mega," the Groover called out softly and O'Neil stopped so suddenly that Juliet bumped into him.

"What ... ?" she began but Mega Trix shushed her.

"Lead on Groover," Mega whispered softly, then took Juliet's hand and led her away from the road, following the Groover into the forest.

Twigs and small branches scratched at Juliet's arms and face and pulled at her clothes. After about a dozen paces Mega pulled her down onto her hands and knees and made her crawl along. She almost screamed when she felt something small and hairy with many legs run across her hand but she stayed quiet and crawled.

"Okay Space Angel," Mega Trix said, "you can sit back and relax for a while. We're in an office of Adventures Unlimited, the most distant office, right on the edge of the Known Forest."

Juliet stayed near the sound of Mega's voice, sat with her back against a tree trunk and tried not to think about all the little crawling things that might be near her in the dark.

The rest of the gang crawled into the office and sat around, Juliet couldn't see them but she felt that they were close by. After a little while she heard one of the bags being opened and then a packet of chocolate crispels was passed around, followed by a bottle of fizzpop. Yellow spotted fizzpop by the taste of it. They all had a crispel and a swig from the bottle and settled down for the night, laying close to each other for warmth and for comfort.

The Plain of Pain

"Wakey! Wakey! Rise and shine!" called out a sickeningly cheery voice.

Juliet tried to open her eyes but found that they were stuck together with the sandy gunge that always appeared when she hadn't slept well. Today she ached all over and felt like she had only gone to sleep about five minutes ago.

"Wassamatter?" she mumbled while rubbing the goop from her eyes. Eventually she managed to get them open.

The 'office' was dark and dingy and much smaller than 'headquarters', barely enough room for the whole gang.

"It's an hour after dawn," Slam Dunk explained, "we should have been on our way ages ago."

"Dawn?" said Juliet muzzily, "but that's the middle of the night."

"Rubbish," said Slider from her other side. The Space Angel turned to her and was handed a double whammy sandwich and a carton of fresh grolly juice. "Breakfast," Slider informed her, "eat up, Mega Trix will be annoyed if we don't get moving soon."

Juliet noticed that she was actually very hungry and began chomping on the sandwich and slurping down the grolly juice.

"By the way," she said around a mouthful of double whammy, "how could the Groover find this place in the dark? I couldn't even see my own feet."

"It's a talent," Slam Dunk told her, with a little envy, she thought. "The Groover always knows where he is and where he is going. He can't get lost." Slam lowered his voice and added, "at least, not so far."

"Why do you say that?" Juliet didn't really want to know but asked anyway.

"Because," Slider chimed in, "this is the furthest any of us has been and soon we're going to be in unknown territory." Then she grinned, "I'm really beginning to enjoy this!"

"Yeah," agreed Slam Dunk sarcastically, "me too."

As soon as she had finished eating, Juliet followed the other two out of the office to join the rest of the gang, once again hiding behind a tree and looking out along the road. Juliet sneaked up beside Mega Trix.

"What are you looking for?" she whispered.

"Actually," Mega Trix whispered back, looked quickly from side to side, then changed to a normal tone of voice, "absolutely nothing." He grinned at Juliet and rolled out of the way as she tried to hit him. Everyone laughed and the dreary mood that had hung over from the previous day lifted slightly.

Although the Sun had only been up a little over an hour, already the day was warm and bright. Juliet breathed in deeply and smelled the tang that promised a hot day to come.

"Come on then," Mega Trix called out brightly, "let's get this show on the road."

The gang, with Juliet, scrambled out of the Known Forest, onto the Road to Nowhere and began walking northwards in reasonably high spirits.

A half an hour later those high spirits disappeared as the road led them out of the forest and onto a wide, grassy plain that undulated away to the horizon all around. They could see the ribbon of road cutting through the grassland for miles and miles and they stopped, as if some invisible barrier prevented them all from going any further.

"This is it," said Mega Trix dramatically, "the Plain of Pain." A collective shudder ran through the group and they stepped a pace closer.

"Why is it called the Plain of Pain?" Juliet asked Slider.

Slider waved her arm vaguely around;

"Look at it," she said, "miles of nothing but grass. Nowhere to shelter from the sun, nowhere to hide, no food or water and it's going to take us days to get to the other side. It sure isn't the plain of fun."

"And," Slam Dunk added darkly, "there are grass snakes."

"Now stop that," Mega Trix interrupted quickly, "no one has seen a grass snake for years and Vizrah Khan says that they are extinct."

"Didn't he also say," put in Flip.

"That Space Angels don't exist?" finished Slip.

"Anyway," Anyway couldn't resist the opportunity, "the largest grass snake ever reported was only a thousand feet long. I could kill one of them on my own."

At that the others burst out laughing.

"What's the matter?" Anyway asked indignantly, "what's so funny? I've taken on bigger monsters than that. Didn't I ever tell you about the time I came across the Gargantuan Horror Beast? All I had with me ... "

"All right Anyway," the Groover was the first to stop himself laughing, "all right. If we come across any grass snakes you can have first crack at them. Just save your story for another time. We've got to get walking."

Gradually they all stopped laughing, pushed through the imaginary barrier and began the long walk across the Plain of Pain, chuckling and giggling now and again at the thought of Anyway taking on any kind of monster.

The sun was beating down, the road shimmered in the heat, the air was dry, dusty and burning hot. The initial cheerfulness was quickly boiled out of them. By mid-morning they had to stop for a rest, a snack and a drink. But there was no shade from the sun, they didn't get much rest and they drank more than they should have.

They trudged on again. Very soon the forest was out of sight and everyone began to feel like they weren't moving, one blade of tall grass was much the same as another and the road was unchanging as far as the eye could see. Their steps became shorter, their feet dragged along the ground. Shoulders sagging, heads drooping they stopped for another rest at noon.

Still there was no break from the sun and heat. Now the gang was feeling almost permanently thirsty, continually passing the bottles of fizz pop around.

Off they went again but soon stopped again. By late afternoon they were resting more than walking. Flip, Slip and Slider were getting dizzy from the heat.

Slowly, very slowly the sun sank down until suddenly, it was below the horizon and they were in darkness. Instantly they began to cool down and all breathed a sigh of relief.

"I think that's enough for today," announced Mega through a parched mouth. "Let's settle down for the night."

Wearily the adventurers trudged a few paces into the grass, which grew right up to the edge of the road. Anyway couldn't see over the top of it, the tips of the blades reached Mega Trix and Groover's shoulders and Slam Dunk's chest. Juliet and the Leaping Lonigans were completely lost in it.

"This will do," said Mega as he slumped down to the ground, "we don't want to get too far from the road."

Gratefully the others dropped their bags and rucksacks to the ground and then themselves. After a few minutes, sarnies, biscuits and fizz pop were passed around and then, very quickly, they had all fallen asleep.

In an hour they were awake again, shivering, teeth chattering, freezing cold.

"Thi .. this is r.. rrr.. ridiculous," Mega Trix managed to say, "it's been boiling hot all day."

"I think," Slam Dunk offered, rubbing his own arms and shoulders to try and warm up, "that it has something to do with it being so flat. It gets very hot during the day and very cold at night. I read about it somewhere."

"Great," hissed the Groover, "if you'd told us about that before we set off, we could have brought some blankets. You know I can't take the cold like you can."

"Sorry," he sounded embarrassed. Even though she couldn't see him in the dark, Juliet could feel the big boy going red.

"Never mind," she said, reached out to where Slam's voice had come from to pat his arm. "If we all huddle together we should be warm enough. With a little help from the Dream Gem."

The rest of the gang gathered in close around Juliet and saw the blue glow of the gem as she took it out and held it against her forehead. The golden glow appeared again but this time, instead of turning into wings, it spread out into a nearly invisible ball that surrounded them all. Straight away they started to feel a little warmer.

"With a fanglefitch," Juliet explained, "I can make a force bubble that will protect me from meteors, radiation, anything. This one is just about strong enough to keep the heat of our bodies in."

"But won't it disappear when you fall asleep?" asked Slam Dunk.

"No," Juliet assured him sleepily, "that's one of the first things we have to learn. Let's get some sleep now."

After their tiring day and disturbed rest, it didn't take the adventurers very long to follow her advice. Soon they were all asleep once more.

Lightning the Snake

This time they all awoke into sunshine, brilliant, hot and tiring even before they'd started walking.

"Can we stop huddling together now?" asked Anyway.

Juliet nodded and 'popped' the force bubble.

The Groover stood up and stretched mightily, twisting his thin body sharply every which way. When Juliet tried the same she stopped as she heard most of her joints cracking and protesting. She made do with a huge yawn.

Gradually the gang got themselves moving, stretching and yawning, scratching their heads and blearily trying to figure out where they were and why.

Mega Trix was the first to work out the most important thing.

"Breakfast," he said gruffly, his eyes only half open, his face pale and tired. "Let us have some breakfast. Who's got the food and drink?"

Flip, Slip and Slider rummaged around in their bags and came up with one bottle of red and yellow fizz pop, half a dozen rabbit food sarnies and three slabs of stone cake.

"That's all there is," said Flip.

"But it can't be!" Slam Dunk plainly didn't believe her, "we started off with loads of scoff."

"I know!" Flip snapped angrily, "but we ate and drank most of it yesterday."

"We didn't notice at the time," added Slider quietly, "but we all kept stopping for another snack, another drink. Now it's almost all gone."

The gloomy little group sat around staring at each other until, one by one, all eyes turned to Mega Trix O'Neil.

"What!?" Mega asked in annoyance when he realized that they were all waiting for him to say something. "What am I supposed to do?"

"You're supposed to lead us," the Groover hissed. "We all came on this adventure because of you. Now you have to tell us what happens next."

"And how am I supposed to know that!?" Mega was shouting now, "Why me? Why can't you all ... "

"O'Neil!!" Juliet interrupted with surprising force. Mega Trix fell silent and she waited a little while for him and the others to relax a bit. Then;

"There's no need to start arguing," she said gently. "We all know the situation. There just plainly and simply isn't enough food and drink to go on. But if you all turn back now you can make it back to the Known Forest by tonight."

"What do you mean "You can make it back"?" asked Flip.

"What about you?" asked Slip.

"You can't go on alone," said Slider.

"There's no point in me going back," sighed the Space Angel, "there's nothing for me to go back to. I don't belong there and besides, with the Dream Gem I just might be able to make it on my own."

"Of course," said Anyway, "I can go for weeks without food and water. I remember one time ... "

"Sshhh," the Groover told him sharply and stood up.

"I don't see why I ... " Anyway tried to continue but this time Slam shut him up.

"Shut up!" he growled and Anyway could tell that he meant it. Slam Dunk was carefully watching the Groover, who was staring out across the plain, scanning the grassland for something.

The rest of the gang stood up, Juliet on tip toe to be able to see above the grass. At first no one knew what they were looking for, then;

"Look!" hissed the Groover.

Everyone turned to where the Groover was pointing, at the same time as they heard the sound that had made him search in the first place. A low whooshing, roaring that kept changing lower and higher, or maybe louder and softer, or perhaps changing direction from left to right. Or it might have been all those things, all that anyone could be sure of was that it was coming closer.

Now the gang could see something that matched the sound. Far off across the plain, the grass was waving, being parted and flattened as if a peculiar wind was pummelling the grass in certain areas. This attack on the grass moved from side to side and forward at the same time, a zigzagging course that was bringing, whatever it was, nearer and nearer.

"It's moving fast," said the Groover.

"Very fast," agreed Slam, "in fact ... " Too late, he realized that 'it' would reach them before they could reach the road.

The noise built up to the muted roar of a wave continuously breaking on a rocky beach, the thing came rushing up and now they could see that it was big, very big. The area of grass being flattened was as wide as if the gang were all walking side by side, the length from 'zig' to 'zag' was immense. Just as panic settled on them, realization that they, too, might be flattened, the noise stopped.

Slam Dunk and the Groover, being the tallest, could see what was hidden in the grass, just a few yards in front.

They began to back away.

"Oh no!" said Slam in a hoarse voice, "oh no, oh no, oh no." The rest of Adventures Unlimited began backing away also, without even knowing what they were backing away from. If Slam Dunk was frightened, then it was probably a good idea for everyone to be frightened.

And then they saw it. A snake, a grass snake, slowly raised it's head above the grass and carried on raising it to twice the height of Slam Dunk. It's eyes were bigger than dinner plates, it's mouth looked big enough to swallow the whole gang at once.

The snake hissed, flicking it's forked tongue out at them, a tongue that seemed as thick as a small tree trunk. It studied them as they stared at the way it's scales glistened in the sunlight.

"Anyway," Mega Trix whispered, "this is your big chance."

The world's greatest liar, to give him credit, actually stepped forward, in front of them all. He raised a very shaky hand and pointed at the snake.

"Go away," Anyway squeaked, "begone, before I destroy you."

To everyone's amazement, the snake slithered backwards a few feet. Anyway stepped forward half a dozen paces and the snake continued to back off.

"Leave us," he said, more strongly now, "or I, the great Anyway, will have to chop you into small ... " He didn't get to finish describing what he would do as Juliet interrupted him.

"Button it, Anyway," she told him, "can't you see the poor thing's terrified?"

"Of course," now Anyway was surprised, "he's supposed to be. Obviously he has heard how I killed the Gargantuan Horror Beast."

"Well, stop being such a bully," Juliet ordered him and smacked him on the shoulder as she walked past.

The snake backed off even more so she stopped.

"It's okay," Juliet tried to soothe the beast, "I won't hurt you. And I won't let any bullies hurt you either," she glanced back at a thoroughly confused Anyway, then turned back to the snake and held out her hands. "Please don't be scared, don't go away."

Very carefully, Juliet stepped closer and closer to the giant snake, holding out her hands in front of her. The snake touched her hands and face very delicately, 'tasting' her, allowing her to approach.

The Space Angel reached out and touched the snake, gently stroking it's scaly hide. Even resting on the ground, it's head was as tall as she was and more than twice that wide but it seemed as happy as a puppy when Juliet rubbed it's eye ridge. All the while it continued hissing.

"Um ... er ... Juliet," it was the Groover, sounding more than a little uncertain.

"Well, what is it?" the Angel, standing so close to such a big snake, was a bit impatient.

"It's ... well, I mean ... " seeing the Groover so confused added to the gang's worries. "Actually, I think it's saying something."

"What!" chorused the gang. Juliet stopped stroking the snake.

"My people are sort of distant," the Groover explained, "very distant, relations to snakes. Most of them are too small to be intelligent but this one must have a pretty big brain."

"Groover," Mega Trix sounded like he was carefully holding his temper in check, "we don't want a biology lesson, just tell us what he's saying."

The Groover went quiet again, listening very carefully to the hissing noises.

"I can't understand everything," he said after a while, "but I think I've got the general meaning."

They waited with an expectant hush. And waited. And waited.

"Well!" snapped Juliet, "would you mind letting us in on what the general meaning is?"

"Oh, sorry," the Groover blushed, "I was miles away. Basically, he's just curious. I get the impression that he's very young, he smelled us from several miles away and simply decided to come and have a look."

"If he's very young," gulped Flip, "I'd hate to meet his grand daddy."

"His grand daddy," said Slam Dunk softly, "was probably killed by our grand daddies. Just for being big and nosy. That's why there are so few big snakes left."

The adventurers were quiet then, feeling a little sad and a little guilty because they knew that they would have killed this gentle creature, if they'd had a weapon.

Juliet continued to scratch the beast's eye ridge absent mindedly, looking along the vast length of its body that was mostly hidden in the grass.

She had a sudden idea.

"Groover, has it got a name?" she asked slyly.

"Not one that even I could pronounce," he answered.

"Then, I think we'll call him Lightning, because he moves so fast," she announced, "see if he likes that."

Being fairly sharp himself, Anyway looked at Juliet suspiciously but she kept up a look of pure innocence as she added;

"Oh, and also ask him if he wouldn't mind giving us a lift."

There was a general dropping of jaws as the gang stared at her in disbelief.

"No way," said Flip.

"Not a chance," said Slip.

"Oh, come on," said Slider, when she had recovered from the initial shock, "it'll be fun!"

"Ask him," Juliet ordered the Groover, who began a conversation of hissing with the snake that lasted several minutes and left him looking puzzled again.

"I'm not sure that he understands about where we want to go," he informed the others, "but he likes the name and thinks it will be fun to give us a ride."

Juliet threw her arms across Lightning's snout and hugged him.

"Lightning, you are wonderful," she said. The rest of the gang weren't quite so sure.

Two Zeebos and a Banshee

The entire membership of Adventures Unlimited sat on the back of a giant snake called Lightning. Flip and Slip had taken a great deal of persuading and eventually it was only the threat of being left alone that won them over.

Lightning slithered through the grass at high speed. Although he took great care not to throw any of his passengers off, they all half sat, half lay trying to hold onto his scaly back. It was like being on a never ending roller coaster ride. Slam Dunk and Slider were already looking very ill.

Their course stayed pretty close to the road, except when Lightning smelled a wagon train and detoured them deeper into the grassland. If anyone had seen them it would have been a peculiar sight, a line of boys and girls zooming along level with the top of the grass!

But no one did see them and by mid afternoon they had reached the other side of the Plain of Pain. Lightning stopped to let his passengers off.

Sore, aching, sick and dizzy, like an overdose of fairground rides. And that was just Slam Dunk. The rest of the gang looked nearly as bad except Juliet. For a Space Angel, who played around planets and their moons, who could fly all around the solar system playing tag with asteroids and meteors, riding a giant snake was tame.

"Thank you," she said to their new friend and hugged him again. Then they all thanked him and the Groover promised to come back and see him soon. After that they were on their way again, adventurers on the Road to Nowhere.

Lightning had dropped them off just short of where the grasslands ended and soon the landscape changed. The road began cutting through fields and meadows, a few trees and bushes scattered around and ahead, already in view, a city. They marched towards it and other roads joined onto theirs; gradually other people began to appear and the gang became nervous.

"Stay close together," Mega Trix warned them, "and try not to look suspicious."

As they drew near to the gates of the city they found themselves part of a busy stream of people, a constant hustle and bustle of traders, business men, beggars and entertainers going into and coming out of the city. Guards were on the gates but lounged idly on either side, making no attempt to keep an eye on who was coming or going. Still, when the adventurers went through it was with nervous eyes and pounding hearts.

No one even noticed them.

As she went through the gates, Juliet looked up and saw a sign;

WELCOME TO THE CITY OF NOWHERE

(Sooner or Later Everyone Comes Here).

"What!" she whispered furiously to Mega, "you never told me that Nowhere was a city."

"Well, where did you think the Road to Nowhere led to?" he asked quite reasonably, "Somewhere?"

Juliet was fuming too much to reply and they wended their way deeper into the city without actually having any idea of what they were going to do next.

"In here," said Flip and led the gang into a small alleyway. Out of the noisy, rushing crowds they could stop and think for a moment.

"So," said the Leaping Lonigans together, "what are we going to do next?"

In the cool, dank alley amid piles of rotting rubbish, Mega Trix didn't have to look at the others to know that they were all waiting for him to provide the answer.

"Basically," he spoke slowly, knowing they wouldn't like his only idea, "we have to get to Ground Zero."

"Excuse me," Juliet interrupted, "what is Ground Zero?"

"It's Vizrah Khan's fortress," said Flip.

"What are we supposed to do there, knock on the door?" asked Slip.

"And ask for Juliet's fanglefitch back?" added Slider.

"Oh no, of course not," Mega Trix assured them with a wicked grin, "We are going to have to break in and steal it."

There were six sharply drawn breaths but Slam Dunk was grinning hugely;

"Obviously you are not serious," he said, sure it was just a wind up. They all expected Mega to be cheeky, bold, even a little dangerous but this was downright madness!

But Mega kept on grinning right back at Slam.

"Oh, but I am very serious," he said, "there is simply no other way."

"And do you know how we are going to break into a place that simply cannot be broken into?" asked the Groover.

"Not yet," admitted Mega Trix with his most charming smile, "but I'm sure I'll figure it out."

He waited a moment for any more comments but everyone was too dumbstruck to be able to say anything. So he set off again, whistling a happy tune to himself, walking with a jaunty swagger. This was turning into the sort of adventure he enjoyed.

Ten minutes later he was in the heart of Nowhere, the market square, with the rest of the adventurers close behind. They had found the market simply by following the direction that most other people seemed to be heading to or coming from.

The gang stopped and stared in amazement. There seemed to be more people in the square than the entire population of Fair Trade Inc. (Which was probably true. Fair Trade was a very small village).

They were all selling or buying or performing or gawping. There was so much going on, so much noise and activity that it would have taken the breath away from most children. Mega Trix Faircon O'Neil however, felt that he was in heaven.

"Hmmm, smell that," he said, breathing deeply,. Juliet just looked puzzled. "The smell of money," he explained, "just waiting for me to come and get it."

"But what do we need money for?" Juliet asked innocently.

Anyway, Slam Dunk, the Groover and the Triplets all looked horrified.

"It's a point of honour," Slam told her. "If there's money to be made we, from Fair Trade Inc., will make the most of it."

"And besides," the Groover added more practically, "a little cash might come in very handy, it might buy us a little help. And we need all the help we can get."

"Follow me, people," Mega called over his shoulder and marched into the square. The rest of the gang lined up and followed, all looking cheerful and eager except Juliet, who looked very dubious.

Mega led them to a small corner of the square that was less crowded than the rest, picked up a couple of discarded boxes to use as a makeshift stall and addressed his 'troops'.

"Slam, we need to attract a little attention. Perhaps you and the ladies would oblige. Anyway, a spiel would be very helpful, Groover, if you disappear now you could come back as our "Lucky Punter"." Like a well oiled machine, the gang all went about their jobs. Except that Juliet didn't have one.

"Is there anything I can do?" she asked, catching some of the other's excitement

Mega Trix looked at her steadily, deep in thought, apparently weighing up different plans of action. Eventually he answered;

"No," he said, "I thought for a moment that your wings might be useful but that might be too dangerous. Oh," he changed his mind, "yes. You could find a small box, not too small, and when a crowd starts to gather, wander among them looking lost and hungry. Can you do that?"

"Yes," Juliet grinned hugely, then instantly gave her best sad and forlorn look that made even Mega want to give her money.

The Leaping Lonigans were getting well into their routine by now, rolling, jumping , doing somersaults and backflips. They climbed all over Slam Dunk as if he was an animated climbing frame and were thrown impossibly high by him, only to land lightly and gracefully and rush back again. Anyway was also doing his job;

"Come and see, good people of Nowhere," he was saying, "these are without doubt the finest young acrobats in the world. See them leap and tumble! Watch them risk broken limbs, broken bodies, even death! Come on Ladies and Gentlemen, step forward and give these courageous young people your support. There is no charge for admiring their brilliance, all they ask is your attention and your applause."

A crowd quickly began to gather, either because of the acrobatics, which were astonishing, our Anyway's spiel, which was equally outrageous. Juliet found herself a box but before she could go into the crowd Mega stopped her and slipped the gang's last few coins into the box.

"Just to let them know what it's for," he winked at her, "now, go and be sad."

Juliet sagged her shoulders down and let her head droop forward, rubbed her eyes roughly with the heel of her hand and shuffled over to the people watching the triplets and Slam. She looked up forlornly at the first person, her eyes now red rimmed as if she had been crying, and limply shook her little box.

The man, well dressed, his arms tightly folded across his chest and a grim look on his face, glanced down at Juliet with no intention of giving any money to this scruffy bunch of urchins. But as soon as he saw the Space Angel's face, he couldn't help himself, his hand reached into his pocket almost before he could stop himself. And so Juliet wandered through the crowd, no one being hard hearted enough to refuse her at least a few coins.

Within fifteen minutes the box was so full it was getting heavy so she took it back to Mega.

"Brilliant," he said, smiling broadly, "I've never seen that scam work so well. But the girls are getting tired now so we'll give them a rest and get started on the big money earner." He signalled to Slam, who signalled to the girls and instantly they went into their big finish, each one standing on the other's shoulders and then Slam Dunk lifted all three into the air above his head.

The crowd cheered heartily and even before they had finished applauding, Mega Trix had dragged out the boxes and was starting his own spiel.

"Ladies and Gentlemen," he somehow managed to make himself heard above the noise without seeming to shout. "Don't be shy, come closer and be amazed. These tricks may not be as spectacular as my colleagues' but they are just as incredible and you could even win yourself a little windfall."

Mega had produced a deck of cards from somewhere and, while he was talking, was shuffling them expertly, making pretty fans of them, making whole rows of them flip flop from side to side.

Some of the crowd drifted away but more than half remained and they gathered closely around Mega, hypnotized by his hand and how they seemed to make the cards dance.

"Why don't we start with something simple?" he asked and didn't wait for an answer. "Here's two Zeebos and a Banshee," he laid the three cards face down and stacked a pile of money up behind each one. He picked up the three cards again, showed them to the audience and laid them slowly back down, the Banshee last of all.

"Just keep your eyes on the Banshee," he instructed the watchers, "never take your eyes off the Banshee." Mega then shuffled the three cards, very, very slowly and carefully, only touching them with the tips of his fingers. Juliet began to panic. Surely everyone knew where the Banshee was!

Mega lined the cards up again, in front of their piles of money.

"Here you are, easy money. There's ten Domos for each card," Mega smiled his most charming and inviting smile, "and all you have to do is pick the Banshee. Who's going to have the first go?"

Out of the crowd, as if appearing from nowhere, stepped the Groover. Before anyone could say a word, he pointed at the middle card;

"That one," he said and Juliet knew it was the right card.

"Whoa! Hold on a minute sir," Mega Trix held up his hands in mock surprise. "You're jumping the gun a little bit there, after all, you don't expect to win something for nothing, do you?"

Groover looked dubious but shook his head.

"I'm betting ten Domos," Mega went on smoothly, "how much are you going to bet?"

Several people in the crowd began smiling and shaking their heads, as if this was the sting they had been expecting and a general air of suspicion began to ruin the happy atmosphere.

"Oh, come on sir," Mega made himself sound disappointed, as if the Groover was the one letting everyone down. "I'm prepared to bet ten Domos but I'm not asking you to wager ten, not seven, or six or even five. If you'll wager just one Domo, you could win ten.

Now all the people around were interested again and silently willed the Groover on. He hesitated a little more and then produced a single coin from his pocket, placed it on his chosen card.

"There you are!" Mega congratulated him and turned over his card. As Juliet had expected, it was the Banshee. "We have a winner!" Mega Trix shouted and the crowd all cheered.

From them on it was simply a matter of trying to keep up with all the people who wanted to bet. And although Juliet was certain that she knew where the Banshee was every time, no one else managed to win any money. And the more they lost, the more they wanted to bet to try and win their money back.

Soon, though, the crowd began to get restless, as people became suspicious about just how fair this game was. Before anyone could get too angry, before anyone realised how easy it would be to take their money back from a bunch of children, Mega nodded quietly to Anyway.

The World's Greatest Liar led Slam Dunk about ten yards away from the game and kicked him in the shin. The triplets let out a joint scream of horror that must have echoed across half the planet. Naturally the crowd all turned around to see what was happening, as did Juliet.

She was amazed to see little Anyway stalking around Slam, like a predator circling it's prey. As soon as the crowd turned to look, he started to shout.

"Don't you ever do that again! If you ever touch me again I'll break every bone in your body. And believe me, I can do it, I've fought better than you with one hand tied behind my back. Khan's own guards, the dreaded Dogs of War, quake in fear just to hear my name. I've done battle with the Megadeath Beast of Rhapsody Four and he only lives now because I let him go!"

"Hey, Juliet" Mega whispered to her and tapped her on the shoulder. She turned away from Slam and Anyway and followed the rest of the gang, leaving the crowd entranced by Anyway's wild story. When they turned around again, the little betting stall would have disappeared.

"What about Slam and Anyway?" Juliet asked when they stopped for a brief rest after having ducked down half a dozen alleyways.

"They'll be fine," Mega Trix assured her, "after a few more minutes of Anyway's ranting, Slam will apologise, they'll both shake hands, the crowd will cheer and everyone will be happy again."

"But how will they find us?" Juliet was concerned by the gang's apparent lack of thought for their two friends.

"It's all right," Mega put his arm around her shoulder and started her moving again, "Anyway can remember the route back to the first alley we stopped in and the Groover can guide us there by another route because he cannot get lost."

Juliet noticed that the Groover had quietly loped on ahead of them and was now waiting at the far end of this alley, carefully scanning the cross roads. She decided to shut up and follow the rest as it dawned on her that it was not the first time they had done this kind of thing.

They ran, panting, through streets and alleys, turning left and right, darting across intersections with the sound of money jangling and rattling in the box that Mega carried. And all at once they had arrived. Juliet didn't recognize the alley, it looked identical to many others they had just come through, but the Groover said it was the one and the gang trusted him. Besides, she was out of breath and couldn't have run anymore so she sat down to wait.

Within a few minutes, barely enough time for Juliet to catch her breath back, Slam Dunk and Anyway arrived, walking casually and smiling.

"You should have seen them," Anyway chuckled, "I had them eating out of the palm of my hand. I could have gone on for hours and they would have listened to my every word. I am, without doubt, the greatest thing they have ever seen!"

All eyes turned to Slam for a more realistic summary but he could only shake his head in wonder.

"This time he's not lying," Slam told them, "he was brilliant. You should have heard the cheer when he agreed to shake hands with me. My ears are still ringing from the noise. There's no doubt in my mind, Anyway, you are the world's greatest liar."

Anyway's smile now stretched so wide, the top of his head looked to be in danger of falling off.

"Actually," he said quietly and with obvious relish, "I was lying, there is one greater than me but I've sworn never to reveal his name."

The stares of sudden disbelief and the sound of deafening silence might have gone on forever if raucous laughter hadn't interrupted the moment. Mega Trix was laughing so hard he had curled up on the floor and was holding his sides.

"He … he … " Mega struggled to talk through gales of laughter. "Don't you see … he's done it … again!" He collapsed into more laughter and gulping breaths of air. "Is he lying … or is … he telling … the truth? Is he the world's greatest … liar or … not? And how … how do we … know the … truth?" Mega Trix was finally unable to gasp out any more words and just rolled around on the floor laughing hysterically.

Juliet thought about what he had said and began to chuckle.

Slam Dunk started to guffaw.

The triplets let out little chuckles.

The Groover snuffled and hissed and then …

Then the entire gang, including Anyway, were on the floor with Mega, laughing and laughing and laughing. They laughed so hard their sides hurt. They laughed so hard their stomachs hurt. They laughed so much they could hardly breath and tears streamed down their faces. And still they laughed some more.

Eventually, though, the laughter died down to a tickle, to a smile, to a deep breath and a sigh. Sheer exhaustion sobered them up and started them thinking about what they were going to do next.

"Come on," Mega was back in control, just, "it's getting late and dark so we'd better find somewhere to stay for the night."

"But where?" the Lonigans asked, remembering just how far they were from home.

Mega Trix shook their box of money and grinned.

"There's enough in here to buy us a small hotel, or a suite at the fanciest hotel in Nowhere. Let's go!"

Stinky Smudgewuggler

They didn't buy a hotel and the one they, or rather Mega and Slam, chose was not the fanciest hotel in Nowhere. It wasn't even the fanciest hotel in that street. In fact it was a dirty, dingy hovel.

Downstairs was a noisy bar cum cafe and upstairs were a few dank little rooms. Mega paid for one room for the night.

"It's better this way," he explained when they had all settled in, "we'll be safer together and besides, we're going to need most of our money to hire someone. Someone who is more likely to be in a grimy little dump like this, rather than the Terran Palace Hotel."

Juliet, Anyway and the three girls didn't seem especially happy about this explanation and seemed as if they might actually have preferred a night in a luxury hotel, with baths and showers and tasty food. This little dump, shamburgers, hot frogs and shiny pop wasn't quite the same. Still, Juliet knew she was another step closer to her fanglefitch.

They sat around and chatted a bit about the adventures of the past three days, laughed a little about some of the things that had happened but quickly became tired and, one by one, dropped off to sleep.

The morning was bright, sunlight pouring in through the un-curtained windows made the room seem cleaner somehow, less disgusting. Juliet woke up on the room's only bed, with the Lonigans pressed closely in around her. Mega, Slam, Anyway and the Groover sprawled around the rest of the room, on chairs and on the floor.

She moved carefully and managed to squeeze out from between the triplets, stood up and yawned and stretched mightily. Mega Trix opened one eye and looked at her;

"Hello Angel," he murmured, loud enough for her to hear but not enough to wake the rest of the gang.

"Oh, 'morning," she smiled and the room seemed even brighter. "I didn't mean to wake you."

"You didn't," Mega smiled back, "I've been awake for the last hour, trying to convince myself that we are not all totally mad."

"And did you?" quietly asked, hesitant, "convince yourself, that is?"

Mega swung his legs down from the arm of the chair, rubbed the sleep from his eyes and grinned at her.

"Nope," he said, "we are definitely insane. Which is lucky for you. If we were sane we'd be running for home right now, instead of which we are going to find someone to take us to Ground Zero. So let's wake everyone up."

Juliet smiled again and the sun shone brighter again.

"Thank you," she said. Mega just shrugged his shoulders.

After the adventurers had been woken up, which Anyway was not happy about, and 'feasted' on rice pups and cherry tea, they all went down to the bar. Which was still open and still serving especially hardened drinkers.

Mega had put all their money into a cloth bag, which he began swinging around and rattling as he studied the bleary eyed toe rags and grizzled old bingers still guzzling their booze.

Anyway walked around the room with an air of importance, carefully eyeing up all the men and women as if they were museum exhibits. Eventually he sauntered back to Mega.

"I'm sorry, Lord O'neil," he said, much louder than necessary, "but I don't think any of these creatures will do. If they had any transport they couldn't drive it, if they were sober enough to drive it they wouldn't have the courage."

Juliet tried to shrink out of sight as several of the more dangerous looking "creatures" turned steely gazes onto Anyway.

"What?" a deep, dark voice growled the question at them. Anyway spun around and homed in on the owner of the voice, almost hidden in the shadows at the back of the room

"Speak up!" Anyway barked at the man, "and speak to me. My Lord does not speak to commoners."

"What," the voice growled again, "is the job?"

Anyway turned back to Mega, smiled and winked. With such a small movement that you couldn't really be sure that he had moved at all, Mega nodded and they all went to the man's table. Only Mega sat down.

Juliet looked the man over and was not impressed. Red rimmed eyes, hooded by thick eyebrows, three day's worth of grey stubble on a chin that looked as if it had been hacked out of solid stone. Gnarled, coarse hands big enough to encompass her head and looking strong enough to crush rocks.

Mega Trix dumped the money on the table with a theatrical flourish and raised an eyebrow to Anyway.

"The "job"," Anyway started sarcastically, "is quite simple. Lord O'neil and his party require transport. Do you have a vehicle?"

"Where?" the man asked, ignoring Anyway and his question.

"That does not matter," Anyway began but Mega held up a hand and he fell silent.

"Ground Zero," Mega said flatly. The man's face registered surprise and tiny muscles began to twitch.

"That's not a place for young 'uns," the gravelly voice sank even lower.

"But we have to get there," Mega insisted, "and we can pay well."

The man gulped some more of his drink, burped and then swigged the rest of it down. He shuddered a little as the powerful brew hit his stomach and probably dissolved a little more of it's lining. Then he leaned towards Slam, placed his elbow on the table and held his hand open.

"You look pretty strong, boy," the deep voice slurred a little, "sit down and let's see how strong."

Soon Slam Dunk was breathing heavily through gritted teeth as he poured a mighty effort into the contest. The man tried to appear relaxed but was also panting for breath and little beads of sweat gathered on his forehead.

For long seconds nothing happened, both arms upright, rigid, not moving a millimetre. Then, so, so gradually Slam began to triumph. Now the man's face was twisted with effort and he grunted each centimetre that Slam forced his arm down. Until, with a gasp from Slam and a roar from the man, the back of his hand touched the table.

"Good," he told Slam and the both of them relaxed, rubbing their arms and shoulders. "One hour. In the alley next door. Bring the money."

As the man slipped out a side door, the gang clapped Slam on the back, congratulating him on his victory.

"It was close," he told them, "very close."

An hour later the gang, minus Slam and the Groover, were waiting nervously in the alley. They heard a low, rapid drumming and Mega herded them all against the wall. Moments later an 'Artic' came snaking into view.

Really it was just a flat, wooden bed, built in sections and hung between two giant millipedes. But they were giant, over a hundred feet long and taller than Slam Dunk. Their gravel voiced man, the driver of this vehicle, sat in an armchair at the front of the flat bed, mid way between the two insects.

Mega Trix tried not to show any surprise but the Lonigans gasped.

"Seen them before," said Anyway predictably, "not very fast but comfortable."

"Money!" the driver snapped.

Mega threw the heavy bag to him.

"And you can tell your two friends to come out of the shadows."

Slam and the Groover walked sheepishly into the dim light.

"You must have great eyesight," Anyway began another story, "just like the many eyed singing ..."

"No," the driver grinned, "I could smell them."

Slam and the Groover both tried to speak at once, outraged that this, the smelliest, grubbiest looking person they had ever laid eyes on, claimed he could smell them!

Mega quickly stepped forward and silenced them with a look.

"We need this man," he whispered and they subsided.

The gang climbed up onto the flat bed, past the driver and found themselves a place to sit. The driver made a strange noise and pressed on two steel spikes that were jammed under the top shell of the millipedes. Smoothly and with no fuss, they were off.

"Oh, Anyway, stop fidgeting," Flip complained half an hour later.

"I'm trying to find a softer spot on this plank," he whined back. "It's just so uncomfortable."

"Anyway!" Mega snapped angrily, "we're all uncomfortable. Surely you've been in worse situations than this?"

Instantly Anyway stopped shuffling around and his eyes lit up. As Mega intended, he launched into another wild and unlikely tale.

"Of course," Anyway shrugged, "this is pure luxury compared to the time I spent two days hiding in a barrel while the Stinky Smudgewuggler tried to eat me." Anyway paused, waiting for someone to ask. With a cheeky grin, Juliet gave him the question.

"What is a Stinky Smudgewuggler?"

"One of the most fearsome beasts you could ever hope not to meet." Anyway took a deep breath and began his story properly.

"It lives," he told them, "just outside Little Dimnock, in a stream of putrid, foul smelling liquid that it uses to pollute all the water nearby. Naturally the Dimnockians have to boil and purify all their water and it still tastes bitter and unpleasant.

The Smudgewuggler itself stands about ten feet tall and looks like a half melted clay Munkstumpey, dripping slime and filth everywhere. Even it's breath chokes like the smell of rotten oogles. And once a month it would take one of the people of Little Dimnock, squeeze them until they melted into a puddle of goo and then drink them like a bowl of soup.

Naturally the people of the village asked me to step in and rid them of this terrible creature."

As anyway talked deeper and deeper into his story, sometimes re-telling especially gory or spectacular bits, Mega and Juliet smiled at each other. Everyone had forgotten their discomfort and were listening intently to Anyway. Mega and Juliet settled back, closed their eyes and were very soon asleep.

The Watchful Forest

Mega felt someone shaking his shoulder and came awake, instantly alert but slightly confused.

"Who? What? When? I wasn't there!" he shouted, before he realized where he was and why his back and bum ached so much.

"Our driver wants his money," the Groover hissed urgently, "but I don't see any castle."

Mega stood up and stretched carefully, Juliet unfolded herself, moaning about the aches and pains in her poor, battered body.

"I don't care where we are," she groaned, rubbing her bum with both hands to try to bring it back to life, "I'm not sitting in this torture machine any more."

"Okay, okay," Mega Trix finished stretching and yawned, "let's see what he has to say."

The gang followed Mega and Juliet to the front of the Artic, where the man sat, patiently waiting.

A new dawn had risen and Mega could see that they had stopped at the edge of a forest. The road carried on into the trees, disappearing into darkness. Behind them were the rolling, grassy hills that led back to Nowhere. There was no castle, or any other dwelling in sight.

"You were paid to take us to Ground Zero," Mega spoke calmly to the driver. "Where is it?"

"You children don't know very much about where you are going, do you?" the man smiled, not a pretty sight. "This is the Watchful Forest and none may enter without Khan's permission. The few who have tried have never been seen again."

Mega gulped and stared into the unwelcoming dark of the Watchful Forest, feeling very much as if it was staring back at him.

"How do we know you are telling the truth?" he asked.

"Because I don't lie," the man growled back. "The forest is a mile wide and encircles Ground Zero castle. The only road through is this one but I wouldn't be inclined to stay on it if I were you. But, then again, I wouldn't go in there unless the Dogs of War were protecting me. Or chasing me." He sighed heavily and eyed up the gang, "I'll take you back to Nowhere, free of charge, if you want. If not, be on your way and keep your money, as it means so much to you."

In the pause that followed, Anyway tapped Mega on the shoulder.

"As the World's Greatest Liar," he said gently, "I can usually spot when other people are lying. He's kept his part of the bargain, Mega, give him the money."

Mega Trix flipped the rest of the money at the man and jumped down from the vehicle.

"Let's go then," he said to the others and they followed him down.

Soon they were in a thick, clingy darkness, despite the sun being well up. They could see only a few yards all around and a damp chill was seeping into them already.

"Groover," Mega called out and his voice sounded strangely loud, "Groover, have you got your bearings?"

"Yes," the Groover hissed back, "we won't get lost."

Mega halted the gang and led them off the road, into the forest.

"I think we should take our driver's advice and keep off the road," he explained, "in case there are look outs or traps along the way. And besides, we really don't want to meet anyone who might be going to or from the castle."

"Who are we likely to meet?" asked Flip.

"I want to stay on the road," said Slip.

"The forest is too, too scary," said Slider, "don't you think it might be best to stay on the road and get through as quickly as possible?"

"It may take longer," Mega began but went suddenly quiet and cocked his head to one side, as if listening for something. "Down and quiet!" he whispered fiercely and threw himself to the floor. The rest of the gang followed instantly and held themselves very still, hardly daring to breath.

In a moment they all heard it, the heavy rumbling mixed with the rattling and clanking of weapons and armour. Peeking out from behind the trees, the gang saw the Dogs of War at close range again, passing by towards Ground Zero. Cold shivers of fear ran up and down their spines and Juliet almost sobbed with fright when one of them stopped and seemed to look directly at her.

After a few seconds he, or she, or it rode on and once again the Space Angel couldn't quite remember what it looked like, only that it had frightened her more than anything else had ever done.

Minutes seemed like hours as the creatures passed but eventually they were gone.

"I think," Mega Trix whispered, "we had better stay away from the road." This time no one disagreed with him.

They walked for a long time, getting deeper into the forest and further from the road. The gang followed closely behind the Groover, trusting him not to get them lost, jumping at every sound, flinching from every tree branch or twig that tugged at their clothes and hair.

They were all very scared, the Watchful Forest was dark and damp and smelly, it seemed to be deliberately trying to slow them down. Their spirits were drooping to their lowest ebb when they saw a dim light through the trees and heard a bitter sweet voice, singing a sad, little song.

"Should we go see?" Juliet whispered.

"No!" the Groover shook his head, "we haven't got far to go now, we're nearly out of the forest."

But Mega, Flip, Slip and Slider were all curious and already headed towards the light.

"Anyway," said Anyway, joining them, "it doesn't sound very dangerous."

So they all crept along, sneaking from one tree to another, until they were standing at the edge of a small clearing, like headquarters roofed over by tangled branches. In the centre of it was what looked like a grumble juice bottle that glowed dimly and gave off a little, very welcome, warmth. Beside the glowing bottle was a little boy.

He was so small and thin, he seemed to be all skin and bones, topped off with a large head and gaunt face. There were smudges of dirt all over his face, snot dribbled slowly out of his nose, his clothes were ragged and scruffy. But most of all, his eyes were sad.

Before anyone could stop her, Flip Lonigan had stepped forward into the light.

"Oh, you poor thing," she said and the boy looked up at her without any change of expression. "What's your name? Why are you here? Why are you so sad?"

The rest of Adventures Unlimited followed Flip into the clearing and also felt the pull of the boy's unhappiness. In fact, it seemed to settle over them all, like a heavy blanket, muffling any happiness or laughter, dragging down their already low spirits until they all felt as sad as the boy looked.

"My name," said the boy in a bleak and toneless voice, "is Woeful Wally and I'm here as bait, to trap people like you. I'm sad because it always works."

"Bait?" Mega repeated, "Trap? That means we're in danger, we should leave. But ... but ... I ... "

"Exactly," Wally nodded listlessly, "it's all too sad, unhappy, miserable. There's no point in trying to escape, there's no point in anything. You won't get away and even if you did, Rip Snorter or Greebo Slobber would catch you and bring you back."

As he spoke their names, Wally's two allies stepped out of the darkness of the surrounding trees.

Rip Snorter was ugly. His pug nose snuffled and snorted all the time, two twisted, mottled horns stuck out of the side of his head, his small, black, piggy eyes looked dead, lifeless. His body was covered in hard knots of muscle and clumps of coarse, stringy, matted hair. But Rip Snorter was 'Miss World' compared to his companion.

Greebo Slobber was disgusting. Long, crooked teeth hung in a mouth that seemed to take up most of his head. There was no hair on him and no muscle, just wobbling rolls of shiny fat. His greasy skin was discoloured by dirt, spots and sores. He dribbled continuously out of the corners of his mouth, the dribble not wiped away, allowed to run down onto his chest, smeared over his body.

The gang had thought their spirits were already at rock bottom but somehow, they fell still further.

"What do you want?" Mega asked miserably, not really caring, too depressed to be bothered by what was happening to himself and his friends.

"I need to feed," Woeful answered sadly, "I need your unhappiness, your hopelessness, your fear and, in just a little while, your pain. I live on these emotions and feelings. Unfortunately for you, Rip and Greebo live on flesh, living, human flesh."

The gang was terrified but lacked the will to fight. Sadness smothered them, such a heavy weight of hopelessness pressed down on them that they were unable to do anything.

Slam Dunk wanted to hit someone but couldn't work up the energy and besides, he knew it would be a complete waste of effort. Anyway couldn't think of any worthwhile lies and Mega's clever talk seemed to have completely left him.

"It's all over," hissed the Groover and the Leaping Lonigans hugged each other, sobbing quietly.

Woeful Wally looked at them all and almost smiled, hungrily flicked his eyes from one to another, feeding off their despair. Until his eyes came to rest on the Space Angel.

She was smirking! A cheeky little half smile that seemed to say; "Ha ha, you can't get me." There was a faint, golden shimmer around her head that Woeful noticed as her smirk widened into a big, cheesy grin.

Juliet stepped forward a pace and Wally stepped back. He fed on loneliness, sadness, despair. Happiness, joy and fun caused him pain and he didn't like that, not at all.

The Space Angel kept on staring at him and smiling, as she held the DreamGem to her head. The golden glow expanded, spreading out further and further, gathering in the rest of the gang, one by one. As the glow surrounded each of the others their drooping heads and sagging shoulders straightened up with a snap! They all shook their heads and blinked their eyes furiously, as if they had woken suddenly from a deep sleep.

"What happened?" asked Mega, the first one to pull himself together enough to ask.

"It's him," Juliet pointed at Wally, "he was drowning your minds in sorrow and despair, so that you couldn't fight back against his nasty partners. They would have eaten our bodies and he would have eaten our minds and souls."

Mega looked again at Wally, Rip and Greebo, feeling sick inside.

"So why didn't it affect you?"

"The DreamGem," Juliet told him, still grinning hugely, "it warned me and now it's helping me."

"What are you waiting around for?" Wally screamed at his partners. "If you want dinner today, get the little blond!"

The two uglies circled around, approaching the gang from either side.

Careful to stay inside the golden glow, Slam Dunk squared up to Greebo Slobber, bunching his big hands into strong, hard fists. Slam was probably the gentlest one in the gang but, when he had to, he could hit seriously hard.

"Greebo," Slam spoke in a low, warning tone. "Greebo, if you want to start losing teeth out of that ugly mouth of yours, just come closer. If not, then walk away."

"The same goes for you," echoed Anyway, who had gone to stand in front of Rip Snorter. Anyway was standing on one leg and holding his arms in a strange position. "I warn you, I hold rainbow belts in Fibarty, Lieism and Organic Fertilizer."

The two people eaters looked at each other, confused, uncertain. It was a long time since they had taken on anyone who could fight back. And Slam Dunk looked big and dangerous.

"We don't have to do this," Juliet spoke up again, "all we have to do is be happy. Don't you see? Laughter is pure poison to Woeful! Somebody tell a joke or make a funny face, or something!"

The gang looked helplessly at each other, minds suddenly gone blank, even Mega Trix O'neil unable to think of a single funny line. Then Slider stepped forward, smiling shyly.

"I ... er, I know one," she blushed furiously as all eyes turned to her. "If you keep a Snaggle Tooth Snarley Beast as a pet, where does it sleep?"

No one answered, the whole gang stared at Slider, hardly breathing. The pause went on, longer and longer until, finally, Juliet asked her;

"Well, where does it sleep?"

Slider shrugged her shoulders and took a deep breath.

"Anywhere it wants to," she squeaked.

There was a stunned silence. In this dire situation, when their lives might depend on a really funny joke, she had come up with that!

But then, slowly, Juliet began to giggle. Moments later Anyway sputtered as a guffaw burst out of his mouth and the Groover started hissing and coughing, his own, peculiar laugh.

All the time, Woeful kept backing away, wincing in pain. Rip and Greebo didn't move, waiting for Wally to tell them what to do.

Then, suddenly, explosively and very loudly, Slam Dunk roared with laughter. Which became the signal for everyone to let loose.

The waves of chuckles, giggles and full blown belly laughs hit Woeful Wally like a physical force. He howled in pain and anger, glared fiercely at Adventures Unlimited and then stumbled off into the darkness of the forest. Rip Snorter and Greebo Slobber were close behind.

As soon as Wally and the people eaters had disappeared, so the laughter died just as quickly. The Space Angel allowed the shimmering, golden field to shrink and vanish.

"I think," said Mega, breathing heavily and still smiling, "we had better get moving."

"This way," the Groover led and they all followed without another word.

Ground Zero

"But that's ... impossible," breathed Slam Dunk, awed.

"That is ridiculous," snapped Mega Trix, irritated.

"It makes my head hurt," complained Slider.

The gang had reached the edge of the Watchful Forest and were huddled together, looking out at Ground Zero. The castle of Vizrah Khan.

It was a huge, blank faced pyramid standing majestically in the middle of a vast clearing of neatly cut grass. But it was upside down!

The broad, flat base was high up in the air and it rested gently on the narrow point. On the ground beside it, some stairs led onto a bridge without supports, like a ribbon of concrete suspended in the air. Half way along the bridge it twisted over completely so that it's floor surface faced the ground and worst of all was the moat. Around the base of the castle, high in the air and facing down to the ground, apparently not kept in place by anything, was a thirty feet wide circle of sludge and slime.

The gang could see bubbles rising to the surface of the moat, heard the distant, wet, plop! as they burst. Saw steam drifting slowly to the ground.

"Look!" cried the Groover excitedly, pointing at the moat, "just there."

They all looked to where he was pointing and were dismayed to see the slowly fading wake of something big and fast, swimming through the brown gunge.

"Well," Mega Trix shivered, "at least we don't have to go anywhere near the moat. We'll just climb on the pointed end that's near the ground."

"I'm afraid not," Juliet shook her head sadly. "There must be a gravity inversion in use there."

"A gravy ... a gravel ... version ... A what?" asked Slam Dunk with difficulty.

"It means," Juliet smiled as she explained, "that if you get too close, you'll fall upwards and probably keep on falling up, straight into space. No, we'll have to use the Moebius Bridge."

"Now what's that?" chimed the Groover and Anyway together.

"That!" Juliet pointed at the ribbon of concrete. "It looks twisted, it is twisted but when you walk across it you won't notice that it's twisted. You're always the right way up."

The gang looked at the Space Angel as if she were mad.

"You're mad!" said Flip.

"Bonkers!" said Slip.

"As fruity as a nutcake!" Slider agreed with her sisters for once.

"Okay then, watch this!" Juliet angrily marched off to the castle. Her companions followed more nervously, feeling very exposed, with nowhere to hide.

About thirty yards from the tip of the pyramid, which everyone could now see was barely touching the ground, Juliet stopped. She began waving her arms in front of her, edging forward in small paces as if she were searching for something that no one could see, until;

"Aha! Here it is."

The rest scratched their heads, looked at each other and shrugged their shoulders. They still couldn't see anything.

"Watch," Juliet took a coin out of her pocket and flipped it forward.

As expected, the coin tumbled forward and then began to fall to the ground. But suddenly, in mid flight. it began to fall the wrong way!

The gang stood dumbstruck as they watched the coin fall higher and higher. It missed the bridge and kept on falling until it was so high they couldn't see it any more.

"That's incredible," said Anyway eventually, "almost as incredible as ... as ..." but even he could not think of a lie to top what he had just seen. "Well, it's just incredible," he finished lamely, "and even if I told the truth about this, no one would believe me."

Mega Trix took a deep breath, managed to tear his eyes away from the sky and back down to earth.

"How ... " he started to say something but his voice was all choked and squeaky. He cleared his throat and started again. "How did you know where it began?"

"You can feel a very faint vibration in the air," Juliet turned around and held out her hands again, "it sort of makes you tingle."

"I think," the Groover hissed nervously, "we should back up to the edge of the forest and work our way around to the bridge."

"Yeah," Slam Dunk chuckled, "and we'll just have to take Juliet's word for it that we won't fall off the bridge, half way across."

It took them nearly an hour to sneak around to the bridge as they kept hiding from any guards that might be watching. When they reached the bottom of the stairs, they saw that they had been wasting their time. There were no guards.

Mega Trix climbed to the top step and turned to face the others, very serious, very solemn. Everyone groaned quietly as they recognized a speech about to begin.

"No," he shook his head, "I'm not going to make a speech. I just wanted to say that I think you are all pretty brilliant for getting this far. We have faced a lot of danger but this is the most dangerous part of all. Anyone who crosses this bridge could be killed. There's going to be Dogs of War, Banshee Wailers and Khan himself. If anyone wants to go home now, they'll still be in the gang and no one will ever think less of them."

Mega Trix O'neil looked slowly from face to face, giving each member of the little band a chance to back out.

"If you are quite finished with your speech that wasn't a speech?" Slider yawned hugely. "Can we get on with it? I want to see what's inside this castle."

Mega smiled and they all grinned back.

"Let's go then."

Side by side, Adventures Unlimited stepped onto the Moebius Bridge and began walking resolutely to Ground Zero. Trying hard not to notice the floor turning upside down ahead of them, not looking at the base of the castle and the moat, high above their heads. Definitely not thinking about how anyone could just look out of the castle and see them approaching.

Without thinking, they were all breathing softly and treading gently.

"Oohh," moaned Slam Dunk when they were half way around the twist, "I think I feel sea sick."

"Don't be silly," Mega laughed, "you can't get seasick on a bridge." Then he noticed how they were still standing upright but the world was at a funny angle. He clamped his mouth shut and concentrated on keeping his own stomach under control.

"Don't look around," Juliet skipped a few paces ahead. Everyone else rolled their eyes and held hands to their mouths and stomachs. "Look at me, don't look at anything else, don't think of anything else. Just keep your eyes on me."

They all stared hard at the Space Angel, trying not to let their eyes flick to the left or right, up or down. Backing away, gently encouraging, Juliet led them all the rest of the way across. Until;

"Wait, Juliet!" Mega called out, "look behind you."

Juliet turned and saw that she was about to cross the moat, which flowed past just inches below the bridge.

The dark, oily water swirled and boiled. There was something big, powerful and angry under the surface. Juliet gingerly stepped forward another pace and stopped, waiting to see if anything happened. She slid forward another pace and waited. And another. Then ...

The water exploded upward in a huge column, drenching the Space Angel as she scrambled desperately backwards, trying to get away from whatever was coming out of the water. The putrid liquid stung her eyes, blinding her. It's foul stench clogged her nostrils, made her cough and gag. She stumbled, fell and was winded when she hit the ground.

Juliet heard the gang now. Flip, Slip and Slider were screaming in terror, Slam Dunk and Anyway were yelling at her;

"Hurry! Get away!"

She felt something grab her, began to struggle and scream but then:

"It's all right," said Mega's voice, close by, "it's me, I've got you."

Juliet allowed him to help her up and guide her away from the moat. After ten or fifteen stumbling paces she tripped again and fell into the arms of the Groover.

"You're okay now," he hissed into her ear while easing her gently to the floor. "Easy now, you'll be fine."

Juliet could barely see the Groover, so badly were her eyes stinging and still she was coughing and choking.

"Flip!" he hissed sharply, "stop staring at that thing and get me the water from your pack."

Moments later Juliet felt the cleansing coolness of the water being poured over her face and in her eyes. She took a mouthful of it and swilled it around before spitting it out.

"Hey! Watch it," said Anyway.

"Sorry," Juliet mumbled.

Her eyes were clearing and she could just make out Mega's worried face as he squatted in front of her, his hands still on her shoulders. Then she realized that he wasn't simply worried but scared, terrified, and his hands were trembling. She looked away from him, back towards the moat. And felt herself begin to shake as she saw the creature that had so nearly caught her.

'A worm,' she thought at first, 'a giant worm.'

But that didn't fit. An enormous tube of rippling muscle, wider around than all of the gang together could reach, the creature appeared to be blind - at least, she could not see any eyes. It's gaping, black hole of a mouth was lined by horrible, wriggling tentacles instead of teeth, each one oozing with a disgusting green and yellow pus.

The beast's body dripped slimy, sticky gunge that hissed when it touched the bridge. And lower down, in what should have been it's stomach, a second mouth kept opening and snapping shut, a mouth full of pointed, sharp teeth gleaming like razors.

"Thank you," she murmured to Mega, still watching the swaying, blindly searching head and the waving, grasping tentacles. "Thank you for saving me."

Mega Trix helped her to her feet, held her steady on knees that seemed to have turned to jelly.

"Wowee!" exclaimed Anyway, wrinkling up his nose, "you smell worse than a Zumzigger that's been eating too many nufnits. Almost as bad as a Jum-Bum twirler just before his yearly bath. Bad enough to frighten away even a wild rimp stickler. I haven't smelled anything that bad since ... "

"All right already, Anyway," snapped Mega, "we get the message. Let's just forget about the smell and try to figure out how to get past this thing."

"We can't!" Anyway snapped back and everyone looked at him in surprise. Anyway angry? Or just very scared?

Flip came up beside him and took his arm.

"How do you know?" she asked gently, "we've got past a lot of other things to get here."

"This is different," Anyway answered slowly, taking a deep, shuddering breath, "this is the Grungeoid. It can't see, it can't hear, it can't smell. But somehow it knows. It knows who to let across and who to feed to it's own stomach. You can't talk to it, or fool it, or even touch it unless you want to see your hands melt."

"If you know so much about this thing," the Groover hissed angrily, "why didn't you tell us right at the start?"

"Would it have stopped anyone from getting this far?" Anyway asked and: "Besides, I didn't really believe it. I usually know a lie when I hear it but this time I was wrong."

The Space Angel stood up, her eyes still red and sore but she could see okay now. She took a couple of paces forward and stopped, staring at the Grungeoid then turned, facing Adventures

Unlimited. Watching Anyway.

"There is nothing that cannot be beaten," she told them calmly. "And I'm surprised at you, Anyway. I thought you were ready and willing to take on the world but here you are, giving up because of one ugly worm. I'm not going to give up because I can't. What about the rest of you?"

Mega stepped forward, glanced back at the rest of the gang - who all nodded, giving him permission to speak for all of them.

"We're not giving up, Juliet," he said, "but how can we get past the Grungeoid? We want to help you, just tell us how."

The Space Angel turned back to the creature, watching it silently as it blindly waved back and forth, searching. Without thinking, Juliet took hold of the DreamGem and a trickle of golden light appeared around her. At once the Grungeoid stopped searching and focused on her.

"Quickly," Anyway whispered from behind her, "Flip, Slip and Slider go over that side and distract it."

The three lonigans crept along one side of the bridge, while Anyway slipped quietly along the other side.

Suddenly the beast turned away from Juliet and swooped at the triplets who, just as quickly, exploded into action. Tumbling and jumping, spinning and rolling, criss crossing over each other, the Leaping Lonigans stayed just out of reach of the Grungeoid.

While the monster darted at the girls, trying to keep track of them, now and again missing one of them by no more than an inch: Anyway crept closer to the moat. Then, without warning, he burst into a flat out run past the beast.

"No!" cried Juliet, "you won't make it!" but Anyway ran on.

The Grungeoid ignored the triplets and paused a moment, as if listening for something in its head. Then, like a foul and dirty bolt of lightning, turned and struck at Anyway, who had almost made it across.

But the creature was too fast and a snaking tentacle caught him by the leg, lifting him high up into the air as more tentacles wrapped around his arms and legs.

"No!" Juliet screamed in anguish, "No! Nooo!"

As she screamed, still tightly squeezing the DreamGem, the trickle of light around her grew brighter and more intense.

"Anyway!" the triplets yelled out together, sobbing.

"Help him! Help him!" Mega bellowed at no one in particular. The monster paid no heed to anyone and started to curl it's head down, moving a fiercely struggling Anyway to the mouth in it's stomach.

"No!" Juliet cried out once more, "you will not!"

The light around her grew brighter and brighter, thicker and thicker until it was bubbling like hot liquid.

Anyway was almost in the creature's mouth when, from the light around Juliet, a beam of golden flame leapt forward and splashed against the monster's hide, searing away gunge and blackening it's skin. The Grungeoid flicked around in pain and surprise, letting go of Anyway who hit the ground with a sickening THUD!

For several seconds the beast faced Juliet, as if it were unsure of what to do now. With the light still bubbling, Juliet said again, angrily and viciously;

"NO!"

More golden flame burst over the Grungeoid, hissing and sending up clouds of smoke where it hit the creature. At once the monster shrieked like the high pitched wail of a siren and dived deep into the moat, racing away from this little angel who could hurt him so much.

"Quickly!" Mega Trix ordered the stunned gang, "now's our chance to get across."

He shoved Juliet until she began running on her own, stayed behind to herd the others along and they all rushed over the moat, Slam Dunk stopping to pick up Anyway. Across the other side they all kept on running until they had reached the gates of Ground Zero Castle, well out of reach of the monster in the moat, should it decide to return. Slam gently laid Anyway on the ground.

Juliet and Mega bent down beside him, gingerly pulling his tattered clothes away from the many cuts and burns on his body.

"Anyway," said Anyway in a croaky voice, wincing with the pain, "this reminds me of the time I fought the Great White Snuffle Beast, bare handed and alone." He looked up at his friends who, for once, didn't interrupt, smiled and finished. "As I remember it, he beat me as well."

"Oh, Anyway you stupid idiot," Juliet sniffed as tears ran down her cheeks, "why did you do that? You could have been killed."

Anyway gritted his teeth against a wave of pain, panting heavily for a few moments until he had it under control again.

"Listen to me," he ignored her question, "Slam should be able to push the gates open. There won't be any guards, Khan doesn't expect anyone to get past the Grungeoid. Now's your chance, get inside and get your Fanglefitch. I'll rest here."

"We can't just leave you ... " Juliet started to protest but Slider interrupted firmly;

"Yes you can. If you don't go in, Anyway is suffering all this pain for nothing. Leave all your packs here and just go. I'll stay and look after Anyway."

Juliet looked doubtful but Mega stood up, nodding his head.

"She's right," he said, "if we don't go on, it would be like we were laughing at Anyway and all he has done. Besides, if we go back, we have to cross the moat again."

"But ... but ... " Juliet sniffled and sobbed.

"No buts," Mega Trix told her harshly. "We go. Now. Slam, get to work on those doors. Everyone else, dump your packs and help Slam."

Vizrah Khan

Slam Dunk pushed against the gates of Ground Zero Castle, the muscles on his arms, shoulders and legs bulging out as he put in a huge effort. But the gates were ten times the height of a man and wide enough for the Dogs of War to ride through six abreast. They were made from solid ironwood and covered in megasteel monsters, beasts and uglies.

Sweat ran down Slam's face and arms but still the gates wouldn't move. Flip joined him and then Slip. The Groover dropped his pack and came to help, along with Mega. Finally Juliet joined in and they all pushed together, grunting and groaning with the effort, screwing up their faces as they strained as hard as they could.

At first nothing seemed to happen. Then;

"It's moving!" panted Slam, "give it everything you've got."

From somewhere inside each of them, they dredged up a little more effort, strained that little more, pushed that little harder. Now they all knew that one of the giant gates was moving because they had to shuffle their feet along to keep straining against it.

"Almost there," grunted Mega, "just a bit more, just a tiny ... " Suddenly his feet slid out from under him, knocking over the Groover and Juliet as he fell.

"It's all right," breathed Slam as the other three scrambled to get back up, "there should be enough room for us to get through."

But, even as he was speaking, Slam noticed that the huge gate was moving again. It was closing!

Like a striking Banzai Beast, Slam leapt into the gap and locked his arms out straight.

"Quick," he gasped, "it's closing!"

The adventurers wriggled, rolled and scrambled through the gap without thinking while Slam made himself into a human doorstop.

"Okay Slam," Mega Trix told him, "you can leave it now, we're all through."

But Slam Dunk didn't move, even while they could all see the door pressing harder into his back, slowly crushing his arms and shoulders.

"Leave it Slam!" Mega shouted at him.

"I can't," he replied, barely able to talk. "I locked myself into position and now there's too much pressure. I can't let go."

Frantically the others tried in vain to open the door again, just a little, just an inch to take the pressure off Slam so that he could get out. But it was too heavy and whatever was making it close again was too strong.

"Get out of my way!" the Groover yelled at the others, "move it!"

He jammed his face up against Slam's and spoke quickly;

"Listen to me. I'm going to punch the soft part on the inside of your elbows. It will hurt but it should make your arms unlock. Be ready." He turned to Mega, "You grab hold of his shirt and be ready to yank him out of there as fast as you can." The Groover took a deep breath and looked from Slam Dunk's face to Mega's. They both nodded grimly.

"Here we go. Three, two, one!"

With incredible speed the Groover jabbed his fist hard into Slam's arms. The elbows folded perfectly, Slam screamed with pain and began to fall down. At the same time the gate began to close very fast because of the pressure that had built up and Mega yanked on Slam's shirt with all his might.

BOOM!

The gate slammed shut, missing Slam Dunk's foot by a millimetre.

They all lay on the floor, panting with fright as much as with the effort. Slam was sprawled in a funny way, like a rag doll that has been carelessly dropped by a little girl.

"Slam, are you okay?" the Groover was the first one to him.

"Aaarrgh," he replied, "I hurt all over."

The Groover tried to sit his friend up but Slam let out a yelp of pain and the Groover let him lay still.

"I think," Slam spoke hoarsely, "I think I've torn some muscles. Maybe a lot of muscles. I can't get up."

"Help me," the Groover said as he began dragging Slam into a corner. The others pushed and pulled as gently as possible until he was well out of the way.

"I'm sorry, Juliet," the Groover shrugged his shoulders, "I'll have to stay with him, he can't move at all."

"Of course you will," Juliet nodded and smiled sadly. "You are all the bravest," she looked at Slam, "and strongest people I have ever known. Thank you for getting me this far." She kissed them both on the cheek, "we'll be back for you."

Now down to four, Adventures Unlimited walked boldly down the massive, dark corridor.

"Does anyone know which way now?" asked Flip.

"Maybe," Juliet answered and held the DreamGem to her forehead. The golden light surrounded her again and she closed her eyes, the other three guiding her along the corridor.

"I can feel it!" Juliet squealed and Mega Trix quickly shushed her. "It's very close," she went on more quietly, "above us, I think." Her breathing became faster, short, sharp pants that worried the others.

"I ... I can see the room it's in. The walls seem to slope sharply, meeting at a point. There's a man in the room, staring, just staring at the fanglefitch. He looks ... unhappy maybe ... no it's not that ... " Juliet breathed in sharply and dropped the DreamGem. "He's evil," she said, shocked, "I've never felt so much evil before."

They had all stopped and now Mega picked up the DreamGem and urged them on again.

"That's Vizrah Khan," he told Juliet, "and with the walls sloping to a point like that, he must be at the very top of the castle. Come on, let's find some stairs."

As they walked deeper and deeper into the castle, searching for a door they saw, not really a light but perhaps a slightly lighter darkness. The four remaining adventurers slowed down, sidling along the wall, eyes darting about warily.

The corridor ended and opened out onto a huge space, a vast, cavern like square. In the centre was a tube, leading from the floor straight up into the darkness far above. Against the wall on the far side was a broad staircase leading up to the next level. On the next level was another set of stairs leading up to the level above that. And so on, up and up, around the four walls, each set of stairs a little narrower than the last. A spiral staircase on a vast scale.

"Looks like we found the way up," said Flip quietly.

"Yeah, hooray," said Slip dismally.

They all peered around through the dim light. Each of the other three walls had enormous doors in them but the square appeared deserted.

"Well," said Mega, "we won't get up those stairs by standing here, waiting. Let's go." And he marched out across the middle of the open space, Flip, Slip and Juliet hurrying to stay close to him.

The stairs, though very wide, were not deep and were easy to walk up. Soon they were on the second level and heading for the next set of steps, hugging the wall all the time as there was no safety barrier or bannisters.

Being the inside of a pyramid, each level overhung the one below, so that the gang of four couldn't see the door opening on the bottom level. Out of those doors came a motley collection of frightening and savage creatures, the Dogs of War, sauntering over to the bottom steps and casually sitting down.

Each level the adventurers went up, Dogs of War came out of the shadows and sat on the steps below them.

After climbing up eight levels, the gang were struggling, having been through so much on the way that they were worn out before they started. But they pushed on, another level and another. Soon the stairs were only wide enough for them to climb two abreast and the opposite floor was almost close enough to touch. If it wasn't for the tube that still ran up the middle.

Eventually they could go no further, there were no more stairs and no overhanging level above, just a roof that the tube went into. All four of them slumped to the floor, puffing and panting.

"Now what ... " Mega began but Slip quietened him with a finger against his lips. They held their breaths and listened.

Sounds floated up from below, faint, difficult to make out. Snuffling and grunting and ... was it? Yes, an occasional, low snarl.

"Flip, Slip," Mega whispered, "grab my feet."

He lay on his belly and the Lonigans held on tightly to his feet as Mega peered out over the edge, pushing himself further out until he could see down onto the level below. Suddenly he waved his arms frantically and the girls hastily pulled him back in.

"Dogs of War," he told the others quietly. "Just below us, everywhere!"

Before they could even react to that, a hatch opened in the ceiling and a stairway rumbled slowly down. It touched the floor and stopped.

"I think that's an invitation," said Flip.

"But not one I like," said Slip.

The four sat and looked at the stairs, tried to see into the gloom above and glanced miserably at each other. All waiting for someone else to make the first move.

"Well, we can't go down," said Juliet as she stood up, "so we might as well go and see who sent us this invitation."

She began up the staircase and Mega followed her, with the Lonigans just behind him.

They stepped out into a room just as Juliet had described, wide but with steeply sloping walls. In the centre of the room was a hole that Mega assumed led into the tube they had seen, and beside the hole was a table, a plain table with a small, unmarked box on it. Staring at the box from a corner of the room was a dark haired man.

"Khan!" exclaimed Mega.

The man smiled but not in any pleasant way.

"Vizrah Khan to you boy," he said in a deep, harsh voice that sounded like it was threatening all sorts of nasty things even when it wasn't. "Or Wizard Lord or Great and Holy Emperor! But don't you ever, ever shorten one of my titles."

Mega just nodded, frightened speechless while Flip and Slip tried to hide behind him. Juliet had not taken her eyes off the box on the table and now started to walk towards it.

There was a high pitched cackle, a dreadful maniac laughter and a … something whizzed past Juliet, spinning her around and knocking her to the floor.

"Tut, tut," said Khan. "My Banshee Wailers will not let you touch that." He stood up and sauntered over to the table, shaking his head.

"But it's mine," Juliet whined, getting up. "Give it back." Another Banshee zipped past her, laughing hysterically and she was back on the ground.

"Now, now young lady," Khan wagged his finger at her, "don't start being rude. I decide who owns what in here. In fact, anywhere on this planet my word is law."

"But you can't use it," Juliet looked around for the Wailers. She caught a glimpse of one, or maybe two or three, they wouldn't stand still, darting around at high speed.

Thin and whispery, with big, ugly heads, the Banshees trailed things around after them that could have been ragged clothes or parts of their bodies.

"That's true," Khan agreed calmly, "but only a Space Angel could use it. And I decreed long ago that they do not exist. I do hope that you are not going to call me a liar," and he grinned a wicked, evil grin.

Neither Juliet nor Khan had noticed Mega, Flip and Slip carefully moving apart, spreading themselves out.

"I have been impressed with you all," Khan went on. "You have shown tremendous courage, intelligence and skill to travel so far from your homes, to get past so many obstacles and then get into my castle. No one has ever managed to do that. Which means that I shall have to destroy you all and make sure that no one ever knows how well you succeeded."

While Khan folded his arms and simply watched her, Juliet took out her DreamGem and touched it to her head. But, before she could do anything, Khan reached inside his jacket and pulled out a gem of his own, at least three or four times the size of Juliet's.

"Yes," he nodded, "I know how these work. How do you think I became Wizard Lord?" Juliet let her gem fall and Khan placed his back in his pocket. "Very wise," he said, "we could probably hurt each other a lot with the gems, but there wouldn't be any point." He stepped away from the table.

At that moment Flip, Slip and Mega burst into action. The girls flip flopped and cartwheeled towards the amazed Banshees, bounced on their toes and lashed out viciously with their feet. Two Wailers collapsed and hit the floor screaming while the third disappeared under the two Lonigans.

At the same time Mega hurtled across the room, howling, straight at Khan.

BOOF!

He ran, head first and headlong into the Wizard Lord's stomach, lifting him off the floor and crashing him back into the wall. Moving faster than she thought she could, Juliet leaped up and grabbed the fanglefitch, snapped it into place at her waist.

"How dare you!?" a furious Khan shoved Mega aside, bellowing with rage. He stood up (cracking his head on the sloping wall) and ordered Juliet to take off his property.

Meanwhile, the Banshees had recovered and added their own, hideous screams to the bedlam. Then, together, they charged Juliet, terrifyingly fast.

The Space Angel didn't move, almost seeming to ignore the Wailers. And then, all of a sudden, she was wrapped in a ball of twinkling, golden light. Similar to the light that appeared when she used the DreamGem but somehow stronger, more solid.

And when the Banshees hit it, they found out just how solid it was.

BAM! BAM! BAM!

The three Banshees hit the golden ball and bounced back, fell to the floor unconscious. Juliet smiled, almost as wicked a smile as the Wizard Lord's.

Khan's face was now twisted with pure hatred as he took out his DreamGem again and pointed it at Juliet. Cold fire poured out of the gem, flowing from his hand only to splash harmlessly against the Space Angel's protective bubble.

"No!" he screamed in mad anger, "your power cannot be greater than mine. Mine is the ultimate power on this planet!"

"But I'm not from this planet," Juliet told him smugly, "and you can't do anything to hurt me."

Khan breathed deeply and regained control of his temper.

"So it seems," he agreed, "so it seems. But what about your friends." Quickly Khan turned and pointed the DreamGem at Mega, Flip and Slip. "You are in pain," he growled and they fell to the floor, writing in agony.

Juliet said nothing but scrunched up her eyes really tight and concentrated very hard. For a moment nothing seemed to happen and Khan started to laugh. Then a bulge appeared in the golden bubble, a bulge that quickly grew and stretched into a wide tube that arced across the room.

As it neared Juliet's friends, the end of the tube widened out, surrounded the three and instantly became another bubble. At that moment Mega, Flip and Slip stopped writing and sat up in surprise, already grinning.

Juliet still had her eyes closed as her bubble floated across the room, being gathered in by the tunnel of light that still joined the two bubbles. the light from the two globes sparked as they touched, joined and merged into one shield around the four adventurers.

Khan's jaw went up and down as if he were trying to say something but couldn't get the words out. Juliet opened her eyes and sighed, then smiled her sweetest, most angelic smile.

"I think that's round two to me," she said softly, "want to try for round three?"

For answer, Khan held his DreamGem high above his head and walked to the centre of the room.

"You cannot defeat me, child," he spoke in a low snarl, "you cannot protect everyone that I might hurt and I will hurt many people if you do not give that box back."

"No way," said Juliet, still smiling but a little less sure of herself.

"Then," Khan went on, "the pain that begins now is on your conscience." He stepped into the hole and disappeared from sight.

"Oh no!" cried Flip immediately, "Slam Dunk, the Groover ..."

" ... Anyway and Slider!" finished Slip.

"Quickly, gather around," Juliet ordered them. "Hold tightly to me and trust me."

The three did as they were told and linked themselves together, Juliet in the middle. The Space Angel closed her eyes once again and the four of them lifted off the floor, drifted over to the middle of the room.

When they were directly over the dark, terrifying entrance that Khan had jumped into, the protective bubble silently and suddenly vanished. For a moment they seemed to hang in the air and then, with a Whoosh! they dropped down into the dark.

At that point, trusting Juliet didn't seem like such a good idea but they all clung to her as hard as they could. So hard, in fact, that she managed to gasp out;

"At least let me breath," and they all eased up a little. But only a little.

The adventurers, except Juliet who was used to flying, felt like they were falling forever but it was only a couple of seconds before they started to slow down. The very air seemed to get thicker and thicker, slowing them rapidly until they lightly touched the floor and a curved door slid open.

They were back on ground level and there, just moving out of sight in the tunnel ahead was a howling Khan, followed closely by his slobbering, teeth gnashing Dogs of War. The gang of four stepped out of the tube;

"Hold onto me again," Juliet shrieked and they set themselves as before.

Immediately the golden bubble formed around them, but this time as a long, thin oval that was barely big enough for them all squeezed together. Mega twisted around to look over his shoulder and was amazed to see the huge, sparkling wings that Juliet had tried to make with the DreamGem. But these were even bigger and brighter and Mega felt himself lifted up and tilted level with the ground. Then they began to move.

The young lord, Megatrix Swindlefair O'neil, had never travelled so fast in his life and prayed that he never would again. He felt as if he had left his stomach several yards behind and dreaded the moment when it would catch up again.

In seconds they had flown over the heads of Khan and his killers. In a few seconds more they had reached the huge gates at the front entrance. Juliet brought them to a sudden, mind wrenching halt and burst the bubble.

Mega, Flip and Slip spun around a few times and flopped onto the floor.

"I had to go slowly," Juliet was saying as she ran to Slam and the Groover, "in case I hurt you."

Slam was sitting with his back against the wall and the Groover jumped up as soon as he saw Juliet.

"What's happening?"

"Big trouble is headed this way," she informed him. "Get Slam away from the doors, I've got to get them open quickly. Mega, help ... " Juliet turned around as she noticed that Mega wasn't beside her. She saw Flip and Slip helping him to his feet and then keep him supported as he nearly fell over again. "Never mind," she said, "come on, Groover."

The Space Angel and the snake skinned boy dragged Slam Dunk back to where Mega was still trying to stand up.

"Keep out of the way!" Juliet shouted and they all watched her blankly, wondering what was going to happen next.

It happened quickly and loudly. Juliet pointed at the gates and gold fire leapt from her fingers, ran all around the edges of the gates and WHAM! The huge, heavy gates were slammed open like some little garden gate.

"Let's go!" she yelled at the others.

Flip and Slip helped the still groggy Mega while the Groover and Juliet dragged Slam again. The sound of Khan and his vicious soldiers was quickly getting closer as the gang re-joined Anyway and Slider, gathering close around them.

The globe of light sprang up, enclosing them all. Juliet squeezed her eyes shut tight, clenched her fists together and generally seemed to be trying very hard to do something.

"I can't," she said eventually, sobbing, "I can't lift all of us."

Just then Khan and his creatures came out of the entrance. Khan himself stopped, looking at the Angel with pure hatred but some of the Dogs of War were too fired up with blood lust. They ran past their leader and launched themselves at Adventures Unlimited, pounding at the golden light with their weapons, biting and snarling, trying to gouge their way through it. But the shield easily held them at bay until, finally, they gave up and looked back to their master for instructions.

Vizrah Khan walked slowly over to the gang, halting just short of touching the light.

"So," he grinned like a scanny bat that has cornered a fuzzblob, "you are all together. But you can't go anywhere, can you?" He didn't wait for an answer. "Do your friends know that their protection will disappear when you get exhausted enough? Do the rest of you know that all I want is the return of my property?"

Juliet looked around uncertainly at her companions, knowing that they were in a bad corner.

"I wouldn't blame you ... " she began but Slider held up a hand to quiet her and then walked to face Khan.

Slider Lonigan stood as close to the inside of the bubble as Khan was to the outside. Just a couple of inches (and the golden light) separated them. She took a deep breath and blew a long, wet raspberry. The rest of the gang roared with laughter and Khan seemed as if he might explode, his eyes nearly popping out of his head.

"You will pay for that," he hissed in a menacing whisper.

"Maybe," Slider agreed cheerfully, "but it was worth it."

Khan stepped back three or four paces and called out "Chair!" One of the 'Dogs' immediately went down on all fours and the Wizard Lord sat down on him.

"So now we wait," he said, "and then it will be my turn to laugh."

Juliet sat down on the floor and sniffed back a sob. Another one forced it's way through, past the choking lump in her throat. Then a tear rolled down her cheek, leaving a glittering, silver track to the corner of her mouth. Then she was crying, face in her hands, water flowing from her eyes, sobbing and sniffling. The bubble faded, getting thinner.

"I'm sorry," Juliet managed to force a few words out, "I'm so sorry. It's all my fault."

"Juliet!" snapped Mega, "I don't care whose fault anything was, just don't let that shield fail!"

The space Angel sat up straight and wiped her eyes. The bubble grew stronger and brighter again.

"Huh, that's how I got into this mess in the first place," she grinned weakly, "not paying attention."

"But how long can you keep this up?" asked the Groover.

"I don't know," Juliet replied honestly, "I've never had to do it for more than a couple of days. And then I wasn't already worn out."

A silence fell over the group then as they all wondered miserably what was going to happen to them. And in that silence they heard a noise, like many feet tramping along. A sound like people, masses of people walking, coming closer and closer.

"What?" said the triplets together.

Now Khan and the Dogs of War heard the noise and turned to look in the direction it was coming from. Adventures Unlimited also looked and what they saw made them smile and laugh and cheer, even while they were crying tears of relief.

An army of people from the towns and villages all around, carrying sticks and rakes and brooms, even a few rusty old swords. Right at the front, leading them all was Lord Maximus Swindlefair O'neil and his wife Lady Gentletouch O'neil. Just behind them was Anyway's parents and the Groover's. Mr and Mrs Lonigan waved, beside them was Slam's father. And following them were hundreds, no, thousands more people.

They marched grimly forward, approaching the moat where the Grungeoid half rose out of the water, sensed the number of angry people and quickly disappeared back beneath the slimy surface. The people came on, over the moat, stopping just a few feet away from the children.

"Dad!" Mega started to talk but a stern look from his father made him close his mouth again. The people on the bridge covered it from side to side and as far back as the gang could see. Lord O'Neil waited until everyone was quiet and still before speaking.

"Khan!" O'neil's voice was harsh and angry, his face grim. "You have ruled this planet for many years and we have put up with much from you but this is going too far. We will not allow you to attack our children."

The Wizard Lord stood up and faced the crowd, grinning.

"'Put up with'!" he laughed, "'not allow'. It sounds like you are all getting above yourselves. It sounds like you might need a lesson, a harsh lesson." He turned angry, spitting words at Mega's father and the rest of the people.

"You do not 'allow' me anything! I take what I want because you cannot stop me! You haven't got the guts or the power to prevent me from doing anything I like. And now you will pay for your insolence!"

He raised the DreamGem above his head.

"Khan!" Lord O'Neil spoke again. "We know you can hurt some of us, maybe even kill some of us, but there are thousands of us here. The moment you use any power against any one of us, the rest of us will attack you and your Dogs of War. Do not start something we will all regret."

"'Hurt' some of you?" Khan chuckled. "I can wipe you all out of existence! I can feed you, one at a time, to my faithful Dogs. Say your last prayers."

Khan stretched himself up, straight and tall, holding the DreamGem high with both hands. Light gathered around him, concentrating into a ball around his hands, a golden ball that grew deeper and darker, sparkling and flashing. It seemed that everyone held their breaths in that moment, waiting, waiting.

Then it came.

The children all screamed, the crowd ducked as one. Dark, copper gold fire poured from Khan's hands, a bar of pure energy aimed at the one man left standing.

Lord Swindlefair O'neil.

The crowd roared in anger and fear, Mega pressed himself against the protective bubble and called out again;

"Dad!"

And suddenly, quietly, without any great drama or fuss, there was a shimmering, golden wall in front of O'neil that the deadly energy hit and was simply absorbed.

"Mummy! Daddy!" now it was Juliet who screamed out with joy and everyone followed her gaze up into the sky.

What they saw was incredible. Two beautiful, smiling people were drifting slowly and gracefully out of the sky on enormous wings of light. Behind them, above them, all around them could be seen the twinkling of hundreds more pairs of wings, like the stars had decided to come down to the earth.

The man landed in front of an astounded Khan.

"I think I'd better look after that," he said softly and took the DreamGem out of the Wizard Lord's hands.

The woman landed in front of Adventures unlimited.

"Well, Juliet," she said, "aren't you going to put your shield away now?"

Juliet nodded and the golden bubble vanished. She ran into her mother's arms, hugging her and laughing and crying all at once. Juliet's mother picked her up and hugged her so hard she could hardly breath, then put her down and smiled at her;

"Daughter, you haven't introduced me to your friends."

Juliet presented each of the gang in turn, explaining why Anyway and Slam were injured. Juliet's mother knelt down beside the two and held her hands out over them.

Gentle gold flowed from the older Space Angel and bathed Slam and Anyway in light. Almost immediately both of them were able to stand up, still battered, bruised and burned but much better.

"Rest for a few days and you'll be fine," Juliet's mum told them and they nodded their thanks.

As the children returned to their families, the crowd let out a mighty roar and the 'Great Khan scuttled back to cower in the doorway of his castle with the terrified Dogs of War.

"We've been searching everywhere for you," now Juliet's father hugged her, "every planet in the Solar System. We were so worried." He smiled and stroked her hair. "But it's all right now, now that we have you back." He frowned, "we'll talk about what you were doing on this planet later," but she saw the glint of laughter in his eyes.

He put his daughter down and turned to Lord O'Neil.

"You are a brave man," he held out his hand and O'neil returned the gesture. "It was easy for me, I knew he couldn't hurt me. But you only had your courage to protect you. I don't know if I would have been so brave in your position."

Lord O'Neil smiled and shook his head.

"We are all a lot braver than we might think, when it comes to protecting our children. Thank you."

"Thank you," said Juliet's mother and father together.

The three Space Angels held hands and golden light glittered all about them. Giant wings appeared and they lifted slowly into the sky. Juliet looked down and saw Mega Trix waving sadly.

"I'll be back soon!" she called out, "and I'll show you how to fly!"

THE END.

If you enjoyed reading this then please leave a review on Amazon. I read every review and they help new readers to discover my books.

Printed in Great Britain
by Amazon